LOVE UNDER TWO FLYBOYS

Lusty, Texas 4

Cara Covington

MENAGE EVERLASTING

Siren Publishing, Inc.
www.SirenPublishing.com

A SIREN PUBLISHING BOOK
IMPRINT: Ménage Everlasting

LOVE UNDER TWO FLYBOYS
Copyright © 2011 by Cara Covington

ISBN-10: 1-61034-855-9
ISBN-13: 978-1-61034-855-3

First Printing: August 2011

Cover design by *Les Byerley*
All art and logo copyright © 2011 by Siren Publishing, Inc.

ALL RIGHTS RESERVED: This literary work may not be reproduced or transmitted in any form or by any means, including electronic or photographic reproduction, in whole or in part, without express written permission.

All characters and events in this book are fictitious. Any resemblance to actual persons living or dead is strictly coincidental.

Printed in the U.S.A.

PUBLISHER
Siren Publishing, Inc.
www.SirenPublishing.com

DEDICATION

To my beloved, whose ongoing love, understanding, and support allow me to continue to follow my dream.

LOVE UNDER TWO FLYBOYS

Lusty, Texas 4

CARA COVINGTON
Copyright © 2011

Chapter 1

Tamara Jones's heart bumped in her chest as the plane's engine coughed. Her gaze snapped to the instrument panel. Had the red stall light just flashed on?

She couldn't be sure. The engine sounded fine, now. Hopefully that was a one-off glitch, an air bubble in the fuel line. She'd conducted the best pre-flight check that she could, but the PA 25-35 Pawnee B had sat in storage for several months. If she'd had her druthers, she'd have done an extensive maintenance service on the bird before taking to the air.

That hadn't been an option.

Mr. Smith had wanted the plane out of his barn ASAP. She had no idea why, and if the man hadn't been an old friend of her Uncle Goodwin's, she would have run, not walked, away from what felt like a very questionable deal.

You know that's not true. Tamara sighed. Her uncle had been so excited about buying this plane, about the crop-dusting business they were going to start together. She couldn't deny him anything, not considering the way he'd taken her in when she'd been an angry, rebellious sixteen-year-old. Though getting on in years, Uncle

Goodwin still had a zest for living. He'd been particularly pleased that they were going into this new business project *together*.

Tamara had to admit she had good vibes about the idea herself, despite her uncle's record of not staying with any previous venture for more than a couple years. Of course, who was she to talk? She hadn't held a job longer than six months, herself. Her gene pool was missing the stick-to-it gene from both sides of her family—evidenced by the fact her mother was on husband number four while her father didn't even bother to marry any of the many bimbos he shacked up with these days.

Tamara shook her head to dislodge thoughts of her parents. She hadn't seen either of them for more than a year, and that was just fine with her. Inhaling deeply, she let herself take a moment to enjoy the beautiful sunshine and blue sky surrounding her. Barely any clouds marred the perfection of this Texas November day. According to that morning's weather report, the temperature would hit the high sixties by afternoon, with no sign of rain on the horizon.

It was a perfect day for flying.

The engine coughed again, and Tamara's stomach clenched. That one was worse than the first one, giving the plane, and her, a good jolt in the process.

She flicked her glance down at her watch. She'd taken off from just west of Abilene over an hour ago, on her way to her home outside of San Marcos, a trip of just over two hundred miles.

That put her midway between, and in the middle of freaking nowhere, judging by all the open range below her. Brow furrowed, she scanned the instrument panel. Nothing indicated any problem, so—

The Piper's engine coughed again, followed by a series of sputters and rumbles. And then the engine died completely.

"Damn it!" Tamara's heart raced. The red stall light sure as hell was shining now. *Great. Just great.* She'd hoped to sneak this plane home, under the radar, because Uncle Goodwin didn't have all the paperwork for the deal yet. All she needed was to ditch the plane and bring the FAA down on her head for not filing a flight plan.

Of course, if I crash I'll likely be dead, so what am I worried about?

Tamara pushed away the morbid thought and focused on looking for a smooth piece of pasture to land on. Something long and gray caught her attention. She blinked, wondering if her panicking mind had conjured just what she needed, just when she needed it. But no, that really *was* an airstrip ahead and to the southeast.

She adjusted her course and willed herself to stay calm. Flicking her gaze between the altimeter, air speed, and attitude gages, she gripped the stick with both hands and aimed for that runway.

The Piper wasn't very big, and it really was in better shape than some planes she'd flown.

Soo not true. Hello? The engine has stalled. Major splat imminent.

Tamara sought to override the smart-ass portion of her brain with logic. The single-engine plane weighed less than a ton, empty. She kept reminding herself that meant with the help of some wind currents, gliding this bitch to the ground was absolutely possible. Even if that was something she'd never done before.

Time slowed, a surreal sensation she'd heard about but never experienced. She didn't think. She simply reacted. *Nose up to slow the plane, check altitude. Attitude good, level on the horizon. Hold it steady, yeah, watch the numbers drop, that's it, a bit more, reduce speed, reduce speed. Glance up at gauges, check altitude, attitude, verify approach to landing strip, check gauges again. Good. All is good. Closer, closer now, come on, baby, reduce speed.*

The plane was going a little faster than she'd like, but then time ran out.

Grass whizzed past in her peripheral vision as she brought the Piper down that last little bit. The tires bumped the edge of the runway, sending the small plane aloft on a gentle bounce that put her heart in her throat. One iota more pressure on the stick, and the tires bumped the tarmac again, this time staying down. Tamara braked slowly, resisting the urge to jump on the binders with both feet, an action that could conceivably send her and the plane toppling ass-over-teakettle.

The plane slowed, and then finally came to a silent stop.

"Thank God." Tamara closed her eyes and let her head fall forward to rest on her hands that still gripped the controls. The tidal wave of relief left her momentarily drained and unable to move. Spots swam behind her closed eyes, and she realized she was holding her breath. The thought she might actually faint kicked her into action.

No way in hell I'm going to do anything so predictably female as faint. Tamara inhaled deeply. A slight acrid smell stung her nostrils. She looked but could see no sign of smoke rising around her.

In one jerk she disengaged her seat belt, and then pushed open the cockpit door. Since the plane had a total height of just over seven feet, she easily slipped out of the pilot's seat to the ground.

Terra firma. She felt so giddy she nearly got to her knees to kiss the ground. That last spurt of relief galvanized her. Slamming the door, she rounded the wing and headed toward the engine compartment. The Piper either had some massively clogged fuel lines or it had suffered a major engine malfunction. Either way, Tamara had a potential mess on her hands.

She took in the area around her, including the hangars and one building under construction about a quarter mile or so to the south. As she watched, a couple of people ran toward a Jeep parked beside one of the hangars.

Tamara shook her head. "Okay, let's see what we have happening under your hood, you bitch." Relief had given way to anger and anxiety.

She had no doubt whatsoever that Jeep would be heading her way. She just hoped whoever the hell those folks were, they didn't work for the FAA.

* * * *

Morgan took in the progress they'd made in two short days. Since the concrete pad they'd had poured last week had cured, they'd spent the past Sunday and Monday erecting some of the walls. The smell of fresh lumber filled his senses. It gripped him for just a moment, the realization that, by the end of the month, their brand-new business, Kendall Aviation, would have a permanent home and, hopefully, be up and running.

"It's really taking shape." He turned to his brother Henry.

"It is. I didn't know how I'd actually feel, returning to civilian life after so long in the Air Force. But you know what? On a day like today, brilliant sunshine and a mild autumn breeze, and our new hangar starting to take shape, I finally feel as if everything is going to work out for us."

Morgan felt one eyebrow go up. "Now that confession of self-doubt surprises me. You're usually always so glib."

Henry grinned. "What can I say? It's a gift. But I do have my moments of self-doubt."

Morgan snorted. "Yeah, like once every decade?" Then he turned his attention back to the partially constructed hangar. "Jordan called this morning. He'll be arriving sometime tonight. He's looking to hire someone to give us a hand so we can get this finished by the end of the month."

"He likes to take his annual vacation in December, if I recall," Henry said.

Their second-youngest brother, Jordan, ran a successful construction company based out of Waco.

"I figure between the two of us, plus Jordan and another person, and our cousins here and there, we should have this done on schedule, no problem."

"Well, I'll agree with you, but only if we can manage to head off Uncle Caleb and Uncle Jonathan between now and then."

Morgan laughed. "You have to admire their industry," he said. "I hope I'm as energetic as them when I'm their age."

"Me, too, but I'd like to admire those traits from afar, if you don't mind. You know, I listened to our cousins complain about their dads needing a hobby, but I didn't fully understand the sentiment then the way I do now."

"They did need a hobby, and starting up Benedict-Murphy Investigations with Colt and Ryder's dad, Mike, is the perfect solution for them all. Did you see Aunt Bernice the other day? She's grinning from ear to ear because her men will soon be out of her hair and out of her kitchen," Morgan said.

"Hey, I'm delighted they're starting a business, and especially pleased they'll be sharing space with us here. It's just navigating that murky middle area—getting us all to the point where we can move in—that has me antsy. I had a hell of a time yesterday keeping those two off the ladders. Thank God Susie finally came by and distracted them," Henry said.

"I'm not too keen on having sixty-plus-year-old men up on ladders, either." Morgan wouldn't want his own fathers doing high work, come to that. Just thinking about it made him shudder. "What we need is a plan. Some way to keep the uncles occupied. Some sort of senior Benedict protocol plan. Hey, I bet Penelope could come up with one. She's even more of a strategic thinker than either Josh or Alex is."

"I bet she could," Henry agreed. "You know, I never thought those two geeks would be able to snag a woman like Penelope. It means there's hope that even a couple of flyboys like us will eventually meet our mate."

Morgan turned and gave his brother a level stare. "Are you forgetting the fact that the woman was *chosen* for them by Grandma Kate?"

"Of course I haven't forgotten." Henry sent him a confused look. "What, are you worried she'll try to ply her match-making magic on us, too?"

"Hell, no. I let her know flat out the night of that impromptu engagement party for Penelope and the geeks that you and I were quite capable of finding our own woman when we figure the time is right." Morgan chuckled. "I think she's got her eye fixed on Adam and Jake, though."

"So what are you worried about, then?"

Before Morgan could answer, he heard a sound that he recognized instantly, and it chilled him to the bone.

It was the sound of an airplane engine stalling out.

He shot his gaze skyward, searching.

"There!" Henry pointed to the north.

The engine smoothed out even as the faint speck moved closer and gained in size. He was just able to see it was a single-engine prop job when the engine coughed again. Then it sputtered for a few long seconds before finally quitting altogether.

"Shit." Morgan recalled the one time a similar thing had happened to him. He'd been behind the controls of a Cessna. This plane, a Piper he could see now, was smaller, but the danger for her pilot was no less. In any contest between plane and ground, the ground won. The Piper changed course slightly and appeared to be coming straight toward them.

"He's spotted our landing strip," Morgan said.

"Plane was flying kind of low. You make him for a drug runner?" Henry asked.

"Doubtful. The payload capacity is too small on one of them to make it worthwhile."

Then Morgan focused on the plane, watching as the pilot executed what he considered to be a near perfect approach. When the wheels touched the tarmac for the second time and the Piper coasted to a stop, Morgan exhaled in relief. It didn't surprise him when his brother did the same.

"Let's go." He jogged over to where he'd parked the Jeep by the helicopter hangar. It didn't take long to drive the quarter mile or so to the plane. He stopped his vehicle well away from the craft. Any worries he had for the pilot's initial safety vanished when he saw the man was already poking under the engine cover. He thought he caught a wisp of smoke but couldn't be certain.

"Damn fool," Morgan said. He'd heard of more than one plane exploding mere minutes after being landed safely.

"So do we let him get his ass blown to bits, or do we go get him the hell away from there until we know it's safe?" Henry asked.

"I'll go. Sitting by waiting for disaster to happen isn't how Kendalls do things."

"I was afraid you were going to say that. You grab him, I'll take a quick look at the engine. Sitting by while one's brother hogs all the danger isn't how Kendalls do things, either."

"Be a hell of a thing," Morgan muttered, "to survive all those tours in Afghanistan only to get our asses killed at home."

Henry grunted, and then they both launched themselves from the Jeep.

Morgan ran, low and fast, and scooped the pilot—he was a small one—and carried him away from the craft.

"Hey, what the hell...damn it, put me *down!*"

Morgan struggled to hang on to his fighting, kicking *female* bundle. Then one small leg jammed between his two and he began to fall. At the last minute he twisted so that he didn't squish the woman in his arms by falling on her. Then he quickly reversed positions with the wildly struggling female so that he was on top, pinning her to the ground out of sheer self-defense.

"What the hell do you think you're doing, asshole?"

"Saving your life." Morgan levered himself up so he could get a good look at his captive. Short, reddish-brown hair in a soft-looking cap surrounded a pixie-like face. Her flashing hazel eyes snapped with fury and intelligence. Full, kissable lips called to him, a siren's song of temptation. All of that was contained in a small, curvy feminine frame that felt lushly warm and scintillatingly sexy beneath him.

"Here's a news flash for you, hot shot. I already saved my own damn life the moment I got the plane on the ground safely."

The reality of having her under him hardened his cock. He narrowed his eyes as he considered her.

"You wouldn't happen to know Kate Benedict, would you?" He glanced up at the sky from which this enticing female package had just fallen. He recalled the woman's question to him when he'd told her that he and Henry could find their own mate. *Damn it, Kate, what did you do, put a hex on us?*

"Look, I don't care if I remind you of this Kate Benedict or the big-breasted bimbo who broke your heart in high school. *Get. Off. Of. Me. Now.*"

Morgan realized there really was no reason to keep the woman pinned to the ground, despite the fact that laying on her felt pretty damn good. He began to lift himself off her at the same moment she tried to buck him off. The combined momentum resulted in their changing positions, with her ending up sprawled on top of him.

She scrambled, trying to get up, but ended up straddling him perfectly, with her crotch nestled snugly against his hardening erection. It was all Morgan could do not to groan out in pure pleasure.

He had to give her credit. She didn't blush or stammer. What she did was push her hips down to let him know she felt his cock. Then she sent him a smirk.

"Just like a man, always thinking with the wrong head."

Morgan opened his mouth to comment, but stopped when his brother came to stand next to them.

"Good news. I don't think the engine is going to explode, after all."

"Thank you for that update," Morgan said. "I appreciate your assistance."

Henry grinned at him. "You're welcome." Then he reached down and plucked the woman off him, holding her by the waist with her feet dangling several inches off the ground. "Why, you're just an itty-bitty little thing, aren't you, darlin'?"

"Aw, hell," she said, "I've traveled back in time to the Stone Age. I never realized Neanderthals spoke English."

Morgan gained his feet. "Not Neanderthals, sweetheart. Texans. There's a world of difference."

"Not from my point of view, and not at the moment," she said.

Henry put the woman down. She didn't run away, just turned, put her hands on her hips, and glared at them.

"Seems to me there's a law here in Texas that says if something falls out of the sky and lands on your property, it's yours," Henry said.

"Pretty sure there is," Morgan agreed.

The woman took one step forward, invading Morgan's space. *How astute of her to know that I'm the bigger threat.* Her scowl turned fierce. The adage, *small but mighty*, popped into Morgan's head.

"I don't fucking think so."

Damned if he didn't really like her fire. It made him wonder how hot she'd burn, naked and between them. He flicked a glance at Henry and knew his brother was just as enthralled with her.

"We can debate the finer points of the law later. I'm Morgan Kendall, and this is my brother Henry. It's our airfield you've landed on, Itty-Bitty." Not completely true, as the field actually belonged to the Town Trust. But it would do for now.

"It's not fair to make fun of people who are vertically challenged." Her tone, all prim and proper, let him know her height, or rather her lack of it, was a sore point with her.

"Fine, then, I'll call you Red."

"I'm sticking with Itty-Bitty," Henry said to him. "Kind of like the way it rolls off my tongue."

The woman sighed and stepped back. "Tamara Jones. And trust me, landing on your airfield was not my first plan for the day."

"Oh? What was?" Henry asked.

"Ferrying this piece of crap airplane from Abilene home to San Marcos. My uncle bought it from a friend of his. We're going to open a crop-dusting business."

"That's a coincidence. Henry and I are starting a business, too."

"You're pilots? What do you fly?"

"Until recently, an F-16 Falcon," Henry said.

"Air Force? You look too young to be jet jockeys," Tamara said.

"Ha. Shows what you know, Red. We're *retired* jet jockeys," Morgan said.

"Awfully young to be retired, too."

He couldn't read the look she gave him then. So instead, he said, "Well, Ms. Jones, why don't we have a look at this plane of yours? See if we can't figure out what's wrong with it. Then we can get you on your way."

"You're pilots *and* mechanics?"

"Trust me," Henry said. "There's absolutely no end to our talents, darlin'."

"Trust you? I don't even *know* you."

Morgan gave her as heated a look as he could manage. "You're going to know us both pretty damn well before too long. But for now, let's have a look at that Piper."

And then he walked toward the plane, leaving the woman, and his brother, to follow.

Chapter 2

I'm Texas born and bred, and still the arrogance of our men irks me.

Tamara would have thought she'd be used to it by now. Hell, how many noses had she been forced to bloody in high school before the good-old-boys there had backed off and kept their hands off her breasts and her ass?

She very nearly laughed thinking of it. The school sure hadn't gotten the desired result when they'd told Uncle Goodwin about her "aggressive behavior." He told *them* if they couldn't control their randy young bucks, he could see no reason why his niece shouldn't do it for them.

Tamara snapped back to the present and watched Morgan Kendall head for the Piper. She took off after him, her temper flaring hot and fast. He was moving in, taking over, damn it. She needed to exert her authority. Her plane, her responsibility.

Man, these brothers are hot.

Tamara pushed that thought clear to the next county. Talk about bad timing. She could count on the fingers of no hand the number of times she'd been hit with a case of instant lust the way she had while bumping groins with Morgan Kendall a few moments ago. *I honest to God didn't know cocks could get that big.* From what she'd seen of his brother Henry, who'd also sprouted a woody, he had nothing to be ashamed of in that department, either.

Despite the not-so-veiled hints from both men, there was no way in hell she was going to do the mattress rumba with either one of them. *Come between two brothers, no pun intended? I don't think so.*

"I thought I saw a tiny wisp of smoke as we drove up," Morgan said.

He was so damn big, he took up nearly all the space under the port engine cover. Before she could think to do so, Henry had gone around to the starboard one.

Don't let your pride kick you in the ass. As long as these two flyboys were willing to lend a hand, she should just let them.

"I thought I smelled something just as I was setting down. Didn't pay it much mind at the time."

"No, you were too busy crash-landing on our property at the time," Henry Kendall said.

"Hey, hello? No splat equals landing without the crash in my book." Tamara's response came almost without thinking, and without missing a beat.

"Hello right back at ya. Plane comes down without benefit of engine, with fried wires, and can't get up again equals crashed plane." Henry looked over at her and grinned.

He's as much of a smart-ass as I am. This can't be good. Then the words he'd said fully registered. "Hell, fried wires?"

"That would be my guess from the residual odor over here."

"You have a clogged fuel line, too." Morgan's gaze landed on hers, and she immediately knew this Kendall was a lot more serious than his brother. "What the hell kind of a maintenance check did you run before lifting off, anyway?"

Tamara could see no reason to lie. "Practically none. I had to hitch a ride to Abilene to pick up this plane *today*. I was lucky to be given enough time to fuel up and run a cursory check. That fuel line wasn't clogged before I took off, because that was the one thing I did check. Everything else seemed fine at the time."

"Those could have been your last words," Morgan's harsh comment grated.

She opened her mouth to deliver a scathing retort then snapped her mouth closed again. Truth of the matter was he had a point. The plane *had* failed, and she had been forced to make an emergency landing.

She didn't want to agree with him, so she just shrugged. When he continued to glare at her she battled her own temper and offered a grudging, "I guess."

Morgan shook his head and returned to poking around at the Piper's guts.

"I'd want to have a qualified mechanic have a look at this," Henry said. "I don't mind admitting, once we get into the electrical, it's more broke than I can manage to fix."

"Well, damn it." She could handle a lot of mechanical repairs herself. But when it came to anything electrical, she was way out of her element, too. "I guess I'd better call Uncle Goodwin and let him know what's happened, since it is his plane." She pulled her cell phone out of her jeans pocket. "By the way, where the hell are we? He'll want to know."

"Just on the outskirts of Lusty, Texas," Morgan said.

He closed the engine cover and then looked up and met her gaze. "What?" he asked.

He must have read the disbelief in her eyes. "Really? *Lusty, Texas?*" She knew Texans enough to know that for some, no opportunity for teasing or leg-pulling—or bragging for that matter—could be passed up.

"Since the late 1880s," he affirmed. "We have a town charter and everything."

Tamara shrugged. It didn't really matter what they called the place, she guessed. "Hell of a name for a town," she said as she dialed her uncle's number.

"We've proven worthy of it, time and time again," Henry said.

"I'll just bet you have, flyboy."

Both men eyed her like she was a piece of prime steak and they were starving to death. She didn't want them to guess how thoroughly they got to her. Honestly, she hadn't ever felt her hormones doing the cha-cha like they had been since that six-foot too-much-macho Texas man scooped her up and laid her down.

Oh, Tamara, that was entirely the wrong imagery to use there.

She gave the men a huge smile, then moved several paces away so she could talk to her uncle in private.

"Hello?"

"Hey, San Marcos, we have a problem."

Uncle Goodwin stayed silent for all of ten seconds. "Well, hell's bells. What happened? Are you all right, girl?"

"I'm fine, and I'm not one hundred percent sure what happened. The good news is I managed a dead stick landing on a private airfield. The bad news is it looks like a whole mess of misery under the engine cover, starting with clogged fuel lines and ending with fried wires."

"Son of a biscuit eater. Whereabouts are you at?"

"Get this. They call the place *Lusty*, Texas. At least that's what the flyboys here are telling me."

"No kidding? You're in Lusty? I know a Kate Benedict who lives in Lusty. Think her family runs the place. Good folks, those Benedicts. The whole town is made up of kin of a sort—not sure what all the names are there."

Tamara lowered her voice. "Would some of them be Kendalls?"

"Yessiree, bob, that was the name of the other big family in those parts. Matter of fact, I had a Miz Kendall as a teacher, way back when. Well, reckon you're safe enough there. You want me to send Virgil on down, let him have a look-see at the Piper?"

Virgil Grant was another friend of Uncle Goodwin's. He used to come 'round once a week to play cards with the other two men who made up their little group, Homer and Otis. Two years before, Homer had died. Last winter, Otis moved over to Florida to be near his son and daughter-in-law.

Things hadn't been the same for her uncle since, which was the major reason Tamara wanted this crop-dusting business to get off the ground. When he'd found the Piper, Uncle Goodwin had perked up like he hadn't done in months.

But Virgil was eighty if he was a day, and his eyesight wasn't the sharpest. It was more than a hundred miles from San Marcos to here, and in her opinion, Virgil Grant had no business driving even one of those miles. "No. I'll see if there's someone closer by who can fix it. They have an airfield, so more than likely they know of someone who'll come out."

"Well, all righty, then. You be sure to keep me updated there, girl. I'll go online and dump some extra cash in your account, reckon you may need it to fix that Piper and take care of yourself. Don't care what it costs. Looking forward to getting that business of ours up and running."

Tamara said good-bye and then closed her cell phone. *Dumb, dumb, dumb.* Why didn't she tell him to send Virgil? Or tell him the plane needed more than she could manage and then make other arrangements to get the damn thing home?

Tamara looked over at the Kendall brothers, two long drinks of Texas water, standing, arms akimbo, staring right back at her. They were the foxes, she was the hen, and she had the distinct feeling that one of them was about to try and gobble her down.

Divide and conquer. Yes, that's what she'd do. As soon as one made a pass at her, she'd whimper to the other. With just the right touch, the brothers would soon be too busy beating on each other to bother with her.

She could stay close by, elicit their help, and get back up in the air and home again without having to surrender anything of herself in the process. In the meantime, she could enjoy being around a couple of grade A prime studs, maybe cop a dinner or two out of the deal, with no harm done, and no foul committed. *A damn fine plan if I do say so myself.*

"So." She gave them a bright smile. "Do either of you gentlemen happen to know any good airplane mechanics in these parts?"

* * * *

"As a matter of fact." Henry looked over at Morgan. He raised one eyebrow, and when Morgan nodded, he understood that he and his brother were definitely on the same page where Ms. Tamara Jones was concerned.

Top of their to-do list was keeping the lovely little spitfire very close at hand until they could figure her out.

Number two on that same list was to get her into their bed and keep her there.

"Why don't you come with us?" Henry gave her a big smile. "There's an office of sorts in the Lear hangar. We'll make some calls and see what we can come up with."

Tamara blinked then let her gaze slide over to the Piper.

"Do you want us to tow her into the hangar?" Morgan asked. "Only one of the jets is here, the other is in New York and will be for a while yet, so there's plenty of room."

"Oh, I don't want to impose."

"No imposition at all," Henry said. "If it's in the hangar, then the mechanic can work on it, rain or shine, day or night." He kept his tone pleasant and watched Tamara's eyes go huge. If he was any judge, the woman was adding up dollars and cents in her head and coming up with a very big number.

"That's what I thought," Morgan said. "Terrence Jessop, a cousin of ours, works on the flight line at Dyess AFB in Abilene. If it flies, he can fix it. I'm not sure when his next relief days are exactly, but I'm pretty certain I heard his sister Tracy say he was due home for a two-week break this weekend."

"Oh. But I don't want to intrude on his time off!"

Henry smiled. "Trust me, you won't be. After two days' leave, Terry is usually haunting the hangars here looking to see if there's anything he can fix."

"Oh." Tamara blinked then looked back at Henry. "If you're certain your cousin won't mind helping..."

"He won't," Henry said.

"Then why do you want to go to the hangar to make phone calls? You said, 'to see what we can come up with.' If you've already come up with your cousin—"

Morgan grinned at Henry. "She's sharp. You have to like that."

"I do like that." Henry waited a moment until he saw a frown gathering on Tamara's face. *Man, she was so easy to goad.* "What I meant was to see where we can put you up at least until next weekend, when Terry comes home."

"Your motels are so jam-packed you have to make phone calls to reserve a room?" The look of disbelief on her face only egged Henry on. He couldn't remember the last time he'd enjoyed tussling with a woman so much.

Nothing worse than a woman who was boring out of bed.

"We don't have any motels in Lusty. The nearest one is clear on out off the highway. We'll take you to it, of course, if you insist. Or," Morgan said, "you can go on home and we'll let you know how the repairs are coming with your Piper. By and by."

"That is *not* an option."

Oh, Itty-Bitty, you sure do like to keep control of things, don't you? Of course, Henry wasn't stupid enough to say that out loud. Instead he said, "Then let's go and see what we can do about getting you a place to stay while we work on getting your bird, here, fixed."

"I don't want to—"

"Impose, yes, we know," Henry said. He already knew where they were going to put Tamara. They just needed to make a couple of calls to get the house ready. "You're Texan, I can tell by the way you talk." He waited, and when she nodded, he said, "Then you know our mother would skin us alive if we didn't show proper hospitality to a...pilot in distress."

Tamara narrowed her eyes, and Henry could tell by the spark in them she was looking for the insult she was certain he'd just given her.

He grinned.

"I need to tell you, Mr. Kendall, that something about that grin of yours just put all my early warning sensors on red alert. What do you have to say about that?"

Henry shrugged then laughed outright. "I'd say you have excellent instincts, Ms. Jones." He put his hands in his pockets and ambled toward the Jeep. "We'll need the half-ton to tow your wounded bird to the hangar, I think. It's parked over yonder."

As he'd calculated, she fell in step behind him, not wanting him to get the last word in, he'd bet. Morgan walked beside her. Henry didn't walk fast enough to get himself out of earshot.

"Your brother, Mr. Kendall, appears to be more than a bit of a roué."

Henry thought she pulled that "lady of the manor" tone off perfectly.

"Yes, I know," Morgan said, his tone appropriately sad. "Our fathers are *so* disappointed in him. They were hoping for another all-out letch, just like me."

Tamara gasped, and Henry turned to see her face. She looked from him, to his brother. And then she burst out laughing. The sound, light, full of humor, and fun, settled on him pleasantly, and he wondered that of all the women he'd ever met, she was the first one whose laughter made him feel good.

Tamara had bent over at the waist, and he and his brother waited patiently for her to get her mirth under control.

When she did, Henry said, "Divide and conquer won't work with us, love."

"It won't? Ah. So all this time, those innuendos you've been tossing out weren't some sort of macho competition to snare the female? Just the two of you indulging in some harmless teasing?"

"Teasing, yes," Morgan said. "Harmless? Depends on your definition, I suppose. If you mean only words shot into the air like chaff from a fighter jet, then no."

"If, on the other hand," Henry said quietly, "you mean that we would never hurt you, then the answer is yes. We would never hurt you or cause you any kind of harm at all."

"That's not how Kendalls do things," Morgan said.

"You two have totally confused me," Tamara said. Her brow furrowed as she looked from one to the other of them. "What is it, exactly, that you're saying?"

Henry smiled and spread his hands. "You fell out of the sky and landed here, on our land."

"That means," Morgan said, "that you belong to us. And we intend, very much, to have you."

"Not either me or Morgan," Henry said. "But both of us. Together. At the same time."

"Not back in time," Tamara said. "I've landed in a mental health facility. Shouldn't the two of you be in straitjackets? And where the *hell* is the psychiatrist?"

Morgan looked over at him. "I really like her," his brother said.

Henry nodded. "Me too." Then he let his gaze meet Tamara's. "We'll just see, Itty-Bitty. We'll just see."

"We certainly will."

Tamara moved past him and got into the Jeep. That action as good as said, "To hell with you both." Clearly she wasn't going to let herself be intimidated *or* easily seduced.

That suited Henry just fine.

Chapter 3

Welcome to Lusty, Texas.
Incorporated 1881.
Everyone is welcome here.

Tamara read the sign as Morgan Kendall slowed the Jeep from country road speed to town speed. Moments before there'd been nothing but fairly flat, empty pasture land on either side of the state road. Now, they were smack-dab in the middle of a town, complete with a traffic light that turned red just for them.

They passed the Sheriff's Department on the left and a clinic on the right. She noticed a museum, as well as a library, a hardware store, bank, and a place called Darryl's Duds. Not one vacant storefront could she see.

Not many small towns had their own clinic, let alone a library. *The little town with the strange name seems to be thriving.*

"We'll grab some lunch at Kelsey's place first, and then we'll head on over to the cottage so you can relax."

"Kelsey, who married your cousins, plural, a few months ago," Tamara recited from the quick rundown they'd given her.

Apparently threesomes were the norm in or around Lusty.

Henry turned in the passenger seat and gave her another of his way-too-charming smiles. "See? It's not confusing at all."

"Confusing, no. Surreal, yes."

"You'll get used to us," Morgan said.

"I'm not going to be around long enough to get used to you."

"We'll see," Henry said.

He turned back around and faced the front again. Tamara opened her mouth to retort then thought better of it. Nothing she said seemed to make one bit of difference to these thick-headed, macho men anyway. She decided her best course of action was to stay silent and let time prove her right.

So far, she was proud of the job she'd done, not letting these two flyboys see just how much they turned her on. All she had to do was keep this up—Good God, for at least five more days? What had she been thinking to agree to stay?

She should make arrangements to go home. It was only a hundred miles or so to San Marcos. She could drive back each morning, go home each night. That's what she should do.

Tamara sighed. Yes, she should, but she wasn't going to.

I like the fact that both of them turn me on. I'm an idiot, and if I'm not careful their bodacious braggadocio is going to turn into my raunchy reality.

No, she could hold out. Then sometime later—when the urge struck her—she might wander back this way again, flirt a little. Play a little. Sometime later when the scent of their bodies even this close didn't make her just a little bit dizzy and a whole lot horny.

Morgan pulled his Jeep into a parking spot along the curb. On the other side of the street, the wide, sparkling window of the restaurant beckoned. Tamara's stomach rumbled, reminding her that it was past noon and she'd skipped breakfast.

Before she could open the door, Morgan had done so. He extended a hand to her, and while she'd rather not take it, she couldn't figure out how to avoid doing so without appearing completely ridiculous or worse, pissy.

Tamara put her hand in his. Shock—pure, physical, and delicious—skittered up her arm, flooded her body, and ignited a hunger that had nothing to do with food. How had she known this would happen? Sensations swarmed through her, heating her blood and racing her heart. Her body instantly recalled the impression of a denim-shrouded cock, big and hard, nestled against her pussy. Her slit gushed with the nectar of her arousal, and her nipples turned hot and hard and begged for a hot, wet mouth.

Tamara stepped out of the car. Morgan closed the door and closed the distance between them by pulling her straight into his arms.

"I've been hard for you since I first wrapped my arms around you and brought you to the ground. Nice to know you're hot, too."

Tamara's hands were trapped against his chest, her body flush with his, hip to breast. The will to deny his claim, to move, to push away, deserted her. She looked up into his obsidian eyes and felt as if she could lose herself completely in their depths.

"We're right out on the main street of town." The weak defense was the best she could do.

Morgan smiled, a wicked smile that sent bolts of sexual electricity streaking straight to her cunt.

"We're on the main street of *Lusty, Texas*," he said. "So let's be lusty." One hand left her back to anchor in her hair. He tilted her face up just a bit more and kissed her.

Wet and wanton, hot and hungry, his lips settled on hers, his tongue spearing into her mouth with bold and brazen strokes. His taste burst inside her like the most potent wine. The heat of his body, of his mouth, seared her. All strength left her knees and she fisted her hands on his jacket to hold on. A part of her felt she was holding on for dear life.

The slide of his lips against hers, the press of his hard cock against her stomach, fired her jets and primed her thrusters. She sensed herself sinking and whimpered when, far too soon, he ended the kiss and eased away from her.

Tamara blinked and barely had a second to register what he'd done when Henry's arm slid around her, turned her, and brought her tight against his body.

"My turn."

"Um, I don't think—"

"That's right, Itty, don't think." Henry's whispered words touched her lips a bare moment before his mouth plundered hers. Wild and carnal, Henry's tongue stroked hers, the rhythm of its dance slow and sultry. He kissed her as if he had all the time in the world and intended to consume her one lick at a time. His flavor reminded her of dark coffee laced with brandy. He was a liquor streaming through her blood, intoxicating her mind and emancipating her spirit.

She wanted more. Oh God, she wanted so much more!

Henry gentled his kiss and then stepped back. He turned to look at Morgan, and both men smiled.

Tamara felt as if she'd been taken out of herself and dropped into a world of smoke and mirrors. She leaned against the Jeep, trying to keep herself from collapsing into a puddle on the street. Blinking several times, she tried to clear her head. Morgan's low chuckle irritated her, but considering the way she'd just melted into him *and* his brother, she really couldn't say anything about it.

"When we get you naked, between us, we're going to burn with the purest, hottest heat," Morgan said. "It's going to be wet and wild and wonderful."

"Yeah, until *you* get off."

Oh, hell. She hadn't meant to let that slip. She'd wanted to just enjoy the flirting and then walk away. A few kisses, some heavy innuendo, maybe a caress or two. Those she could allow herself. Anything more would just open her up for disappointment.

It was a letdown she knew well. She'd only had a couple of lovers, but the dance was the same. Just as she was ready to come, her partner would climax and immediately lose interest. In the past, that kind of frustration had stung. In the case of these two Kendalls, she had the feeling the disappointment would be devastating.

"That sounded like a challenge, Red," Morgan said.

"A delicious one at that," Henry agreed. Then he stroked his hand down her hair. "Don't you worry, Itty-Bitty. You're going to come so often and so hard you won't even remember your own name."

"Let's go, Tamara." Morgan took her hand, kissed it, then drew her away from the car. "Let's get you some lunch. You look a mite peaked."

Tamara had time to look up at the sign over the restaurant. *Lusty Appetites*. She had the sinking sensation she already had all the lusty appetite she would ever be able to handle.

* * * *

Morgan snagged a round table in the back corner of the restaurant, seating Tamara between him and his brother. He needed to sit down, to focus on something other than the luscious woman who'd fallen out of the sky and into their lives.

She'd tasted better than any woman he'd ever sampled. It had taken every bit of his will not to take her right there on Main Street in front of God, man, and quite possibly his mother. It was, after all, not a very big town.

Tamara Jones packed more punch than a jet engine hitting Mach 2, and she didn't even seem to realize it.

Of course he and Henry both understood they'd knocked her off balance right from the first moment. They planned to keep her there, too. At least until they sank balls-deep into her.

He'd know, then, if she was the one meant to be theirs, or not.

Liar. You know already.

"Hey, Morgan, hey, Henry. Y'all just missed the lunch crowd. We had a lively one today."

Morgan smiled at Ginny Rose, Kelsey's newest waitress. The young woman had been a member of their community for just over six months, and it seemed to him she was finally coming into her own. Today she had her hair pulled back with a pretty clip, and if he wasn't mistaken, she was wearing a bit of makeup.

"Hey there, Ginny, how are you doing today? Meet Tamara Jones. Her plane had an engine failure, and she managed to bring it down out on the strip."

"Oh my word!" Ginny's eyes widened in sympathy. She put her whole attention on Tamara. "Why, that must have scared you silly!" Ginny shuddered as she said that. Morgan was left with no doubt Ginny would be a nervous flyer.

Tamara smiled at Ginny. "Well, it certainly was exciting for a little bit, there. But I'm mostly over it."

"Well, I'm glad you were able to land it okay. Now, the special today is Country-fried steak with fries and slaw. Here's the menu if you want to look at what else we have. Y'all want some tea or a soda to start with?"

"I'd like a Coke, and I don't need to read the menu, thanks. I like the sound of the special," Tamara said.

Both he and Henry decided to have the same. "Could you tell Tracy that we're here?" he asked Ginny. "I think she's expecting us."

"I'll do that. And I'll be back in a few moments with your drinks."

Ginny went into the kitchen. Tamara turned to him. "So, who's she married to? Ginny?"

"No one, yet," Morgan said. "Our brother Adam seems taken with her, though."

"Jake, too," Henry said.

"Why am I not surprised? Anyway," he turned his attention back to Tamara, "Ginny moved here from Waco a few months back, so she's still trying to acclimate."

"She gets months to acclimate, and you want me to get used to you in just a few days?" Tamara blushed, and he knew she hadn't meant to say that.

"As Henry said, you're not confused at all," Morgan said.

The kitchen door opened, and a petite blonde, her hair pulled up in a knot on top of her head, practically exploded into the dining room. She carried two shopping bags and made a beeline straight for them.

"Hey, Morgan, Hey, Henry."

"Tracy, this is Tamara Jones. Tamara, this is our cousin, Tracy Jessop."

"Another cousin?"

"The town is lousy with them." Tracy laughed. "I threw together a couple bags of clothing for you. The flyboys here said you landed without luggage. This should be enough to last you a few days."

"Oh!" Tamara's cheeks turned pink.

It was all Morgan could do not to laugh. In the time between when he first wrapped his arms around the little spitfire, to towing the Piper into the hangar, to huddling in the office, making calls to arrange her accommodations for the duration, Tamara hadn't seemed to notice that she didn't even have so much as a change of clothes or a toothbrush. Unless, of course, she carried one in that tiny fanny pack she wore.

"Thank you, Tracy. I don't want to—"

"Impose?" Tracy smiled. "You're not. I'm glad to be of help." She paused and gave Tamara a look. "Henry was right. We are about the same size. Oh, and before I forget, Terry called me about ten minutes ago, when he couldn't get an answer out at the field. Said he'll be here Saturday, and he'd be glad to lend a hand. Between you and me, he sounded eager as all get-out. With any luck, he'll leave our cars be this time."

"That's great. Really. Thank you." Tamara's voice came out the quietest he'd heard it.

"Like I said, happy to help. Well, I have to get back to work before the boss gets back." Tracy winked and headed straight back to the kitchen.

Morgan raised one eyebrow as he looked at Henry. Apparently all that was necessary to render Red speechless was to do something nice for her. By Henry's expression, he'd noticed that, too.

He had the feeling she wasn't used to people being kind to her—especially if those people were total strangers. As elated as he felt to have a key to her already, knowing she'd not experienced much kindness in her life made him mad as hell.

Ginny came back with their drinks. "Here you go. Lunch will be out in a bit."

"It all smells so good in here," Tamara said. She took a sip of her soda, then set it down.

"Kelsey and Tracy are both excellent chefs," Henry said. "Kelsey has been trying to convince Tracy to go after her chef's certification—she's sous-chef here now, and a genius when it comes to desserts."

"Maybe she likes where she is in life."

"That would be one of my guesses," Henry said. He leaned forward and set his arms on the table. "We haven't spent as much time in town lately, having been stationed in different places over the last few years. We'd come home on leave, of course. But it's not the same as settling in and settling down."

"You both went into the Air Force. I always imagined siblings would want to go out on their own path, so to speak."

"You don't have any brothers or sisters?" Morgan asked her.

Tamara shrugged, which in itself was an odd response to the question.

"I have a half brother," she said. "We share a mother, and nothing else. He was born when I was fourteen, with mom's second, no, sorry, her third husband. She's on number four right now. I don't think my father has begat any kids besides me, but I really couldn't swear to it."

"And you have your uncle," Morgan said.

Tamara smiled. "Yeah. He's actually my great-uncle. Took me in when I was sixteen and mad at the world. His solution was to give me space and flying lessons. There was a small, private airstrip outside San Marcos and a grizzled old pilot who was a friend of Uncle Goodwin's."

"You going to tell that old pilot that you crashed today?" Henry asked.

Tamara narrowed her eyes. "I didn't crash. I executed a near flawless dead-stick landing. With nerves of steel, I might add."

Ginny came out of the kitchen bearing their lunch. The aroma of the food reminded Morgan how hungry he was.

Henry had teased the chip off her shoulder. Personally, he couldn't blame her for having one. He'd taken his family—both immediate and extended—for granted most of his life. He wouldn't doubt that the reason he'd been able to do the things he had was thanks to the confidence he'd gained from his family.

"So what is this cottage you've arranged for me to stay at?" Tamara asked.

"Just a little place tucked in at the edge of town," Henry said. "It's been in the family for years. It's not much, but it has a roof and a fireplace. You'll be comfy there."

"You'll let me know how much rent I'll owe for the week?"

"Sorry. Can't accept any money from you. That's not how Kendalls do things," Morgan said.

"Well, I can't freeload off you, or your family. That's not how Tamara does things."

Interesting that she'd just refer to herself that way, and not by her family name. That told him even more succinctly that she considered herself a lone entity.

"All right. You can fly a plane. Can you wield a hammer?"

Morgan could see his question surprised her. She stopped her fork just before it reached her mouth and raised one eyebrow. Then she opened her mouth, slowly drew the food in, and left Morgan feeling hotter than ever.

"I have done, in the past. Why?"

"We'll deal," Morgan said. And as his own words echoed in his head, he knew they'd likely deal on just about every damn thing.

He glanced up and caught his brother's expression. They were a pair of sorry pups because he could tell, looking at Henry, they were both looking forward to it.

Chapter 4

Everything had been going so well until that fucking pilot got greedy.

Preston Rogers ran an agitated hand through his hair as the limousine he was riding in took him along the streets of the old town. He wasn't familiar with El Paso and didn't have many contacts in west Texas. That was likely the reason he'd been ordered here, to meet with Mr. Ramos in person.

Preston had been doing business with the man for nearly three years and had met him only once before. The other times when negotiations had been necessary, he'd met the man's lieutenant—a ferret-faced little son-of-a-bitch named Ernie.

Ernie, for God's sake.

Preston sat back and tried to calm his nerves. He knew giving him a good scare was likely the entire point of this little exercise. At least he hoped that's all it was, an exercise. The message certainly didn't escape him. Miguel Ramos was powerful enough, and certainly ruthless enough, to have him taken for a ride, beyond the city, out into the desert, and left—somewhere the scavengers could pick his carcass clean and his skeleton would be bleached white by the hot west Texas sun.

Yeah, he got the message, loud and clear. He only hoped the news he had to impart would placate the man.

The car slowed and then turned right and came to a stop. Preston could see out the windshield at least. He would have been totally unnerved if the car had come with a sliding panel between the front and back seats. In front of the car, gates opened, and then the car continued on, about a quarter of a mile, pulling into a circular driveway in front of a very large adobe house.

The car door beside him opened, and a man stood, silent and waiting. Preston exited the vehicle and spread his arms out slightly so this man, likely one of Mr. Ramos' bodyguards, could verify that he'd come unarmed.

The six-inch sticker concealed in his boot meant he wasn't completely helpless, but he'd just as soon keep that weapon a secret for the time being.

The guard finished patting him down, grunted, and stepped back. He gestured for him to enter the house. Inside, the long corridor had two more bodyguards, these ones armed with very big guns. One of them stepped forward, and Preston realized he was expected to follow him. It took all of his acting ability to continue to appear insouciant. Why hadn't he listened to his mother and headed to Hollywood? He could act. Fuck, he likely could have had three times the money without any of the stress he had to endure now.

The guard led him to a cozy room, complete with wing back chairs and a welcoming fire burning in the hearth.

"Ah, Señor Rogers. Please, come in, sit down. Rico, please pour a glass of wine for our guest."

"Señor Ramos, thank you for the honor of this meeting."

Miguel Ramos appeared to be a man in his prime. Handsome, well dressed, well groomed, he was a man who could command attention even without the armed enforcers. Preston figured the guy had to be in his early sixties, but could pass for a couple of decades younger.

He thanked the servant for the glass of wine and took a very small sip. Beer was more his drink, but he was smart enough to understand the ceremony of the situation.

"Now, I am hoping that you have some good news for me?"

"Yes, sir, I do." He could draw things out, or get to the point. He'd just as soon get back to his home turf as quickly as possible. "When my people were unable to locate a crash site, or find any trace of Mr. West's plane, I got suspicious. So I had one of my people who is very good with computers do some investigating and then some hacking. And what we discovered is that Mr. West's credit card and bank account have been used after he supposedly crashed and died."

"I see." Ramos looked off to the side. "Mr. West was recommended to us by Ernesto, who, sadly, is no longer in my employ. For this reason, I am willing to give you more time to locate Mr. West and the goods that belong to me. You will, of course, receive no more shipments of merchandise until I receive my payment for the last one."

Well, at least now Preston knew why he hadn't seen ferret-face. That man was likely dead, and his body would never be found.

No way in hell was Preston going to tell Ramos they'd already found West. One of his men had gotten a little too enthusiastic in his questioning, and the damn thieving pilot had died of a heart attack before he'd revealed the *exact* location of his plane. But they had an area, and they had Frank West's laptop. Preston believed it was only a matter of time before this situation was resolved. He nodded to Ramos. "I'm grateful, sir, for your patience and generosity in this matter. Please be assured I am doing everything in my power to see that you receive that payment."

"Si, I am sure you are. I am also sure you understand the price of failure, Señor Rogers."

"Yes, Señor Ramos, I do." Preston handed his glass to the servant who'd stepped forward. He got to his feet, nodded, then left the room. Retracing his steps he held his breath, hoping he didn't get a bullet in his back for his trouble.

He didn't fully relax until the limo pulled up to his hotel and he was out of the car and inside the lobby. Even there he knew he wasn't completely safe. But he did believe that if Miguel Ramos had meant for him to die tonight, he'd already be dead.

The elevator doors opened as he approached, and he wasted no time getting in and pressing the button for his floor. He waited until he was inside his room before he pulled out his cell phone. He punched number two on speed dial. The phone was answered on the second ring.

"Jimmy, tell me you've found that fucking Piper."

"Sir, we believe we may have. West had some e-mail contact with a farmer just outside of Abilene. I accessed Anywhere Earth, the satellite photo site. The man's got a couple of buildings big enough to hold that plane. There was also a payment out of West's Money Buddy account to this farmer—a man by the name of John Smith. Apparently that's his *real* name."

"All right. You sit tight. I'll join you in the morning. Then we're going to give Mr. Smith a little visit. Did you see to Mr. West's remains?"

"No, Dennis did that. He took the body to his apartment. I was too busy going through the man's computer, looking for the plane."

"You did a good job, Jimmy."

"Thank you, sir."

Preston closed his phone and hoped to hell Dennis also had done a real good job of staging West's body. The man had died of a heart attack, and Dennis hadn't done much more than threaten him with his gun. Technically, they were all guilty of murder two, but hopefully the authorities would cite heart failure as West's cause of death. The last thing he needed was to have the feds breathing down his neck looking to hang a murder charge on him.

All he wanted was to recover the Piper and the secret stash hidden inside her. The sooner Miguel Ramos had his diamonds, the sooner Preston and his business would be able to return to normal.

* * * *

"You said it was a *cottage*." Tamara stood in the lane, looking up at the two-story Victorian house. A curved, covered porch at the front supported what looked like a walk-out area for the second story. With its white stucco, dark wood siding, the building appealed to her more than she felt comfortable admitting.

"Well, that's just what we've always called the place."

"It was built by a Kendall in the 1920s and has actually only sat empty for a few months," Henry said.

"Come on, we'll give you the nickel tour." Morgan reached forward and opened the door.

"It's not locked?"

"Well, it was, until about a half an hour ago. Don't worry. We'll give you a key. You'll be as safe as you want to be here."

That was a very strange thing to say. Tamara pushed that thought away. These two flyboys seemed to specialize in saying strange things. Instead, she focused on the place that would be home to her for the next few days.

No question, the house was gorgeous. Inside, a large sofa and three comfortable-looking armchairs in soft brown graced a downstairs parlor painted in eggshell with a matte finish. The trim, all rich-looking dark wood, gleamed, as did the polished wood floor. The area rug, tan with brown and green accents, looked to be of a very deep pile. Tamara imagined her bare toes sinking into it.

The kitchen had clearly been remodeled, as the appliances, all stainless steel, appeared brand new. The black granite countertop had flecks of gold, and it was all Tamara could do not to reach out and caress it with her hand. She was only a passable cook, but this kitchen reached out to her domestic side.

Off the kitchen, a formal dining room stood as if just waiting to receive the best crystal and china money could buy. The long cherrywood table sported a fine linen runner with a cactus planter in the center. But what stole Tamara's breath was the beautiful fireplace, old-fashioned red brick and granite hearth, that took up center stage along one wall.

"Someone has really good decorating sense," she said.

The brothers said nothing. They just grinned. Did that mean they'd decorated the place themselves? Surely not. In her experience men not only didn't possess decorating sense, they didn't even know such a thing existed.

Upstairs, to the right, stood a small bedroom, the only room in the house, so far, without a lick of furniture in it. A window adorned with a lace curtain looked out over the backyard. Then she went across the hall to what clearly was the master bedroom.

Her jaw dropped. "That is the biggest bed I have ever seen! That's got to be even larger than a king-sized bed. What the hell do you call a bed that big?"

"Lusty sized," Morgan said.

The two men stood very close to her, and she could feel their heat, scent their skin. Unbidden, their flavors, shared so freely with her during those incendiary kisses earlier, flooded her anew. Oh, it was *so* not a good idea for her to be anywhere near a bed with these two flyboys standing so close.

Tamara took a step away from them and fought for air. The room itself was large, with a fireplace on the far wall that also featured an archway. Blinking, Tamara realized there was another room on the other side of the fireplace. Curious, she went to investigate.

"That's too posh to be called a bathroom." The space held a good-sized Jacuzzi, a very large claw-foot tub, and a shower big enough to hold a party in with see-through glass walls. She had to push back the images that flashed through her mind, images of naked men, hot water, and hotter sex.

She turned and looked at the two men. "This is *way* too much house for me."

"What are you afraid of, Itty-Bitty?"

Tamara's temper sparked, fast and furious. She marched right over to Henry Kendall and poked him in the chest with her index finger. "I'm not afraid of anything, flyboy."

"Good."

He combed his fingers through her hair and tilted her head up, up, until their gazes met. *I should really say something snarky and step back.* That was the last cogent thought she had before his lips settled on hers.

Powerful, potent, his kiss consumed her, sucking her tongue into his mouth and her will to resist clear out of her brain. Arousal, sharp and sweet, swept through her, a sirocco of succulent sensuality that heated her blood and slicked her sex. She felt her knees go weak and didn't care. All she wanted in that moment was for this kiss to go on, for the rising fire within her to burn, and for his taste to fill her completely.

She felt Morgan come up behind her until his body braced hers, and when Henry eased his lips from hers, she instinctively turned her head, seeking Morgan's lips.

"Yes, give me some of that fire." His words brushed her lips. Then he opened his mouth over hers. His kiss, compelling and carnal, destroyed the last of her defenses, and Tamara surrendered completely. His tongue tangled with hers, stroking, dancing, seducing. A soul-deep moan of pleasure vibrated from her chest.

"God, you taste like more," Morgan said.

"You're very addictive, love," Henry agreed.

Tamara gasped for breath and then shivered as they set their hands on her. Henry stroked back and forth across her breasts. She might as well have been naked, for her nipples pinched, reaching for his touch, a touch that made her hotter and wetter.

Morgan reached down and slowly, deeply caressed the denim that covered her cunt.

Tamara had never whimpered in her life, but she did now, tilting her hips, silently begging for more.

"Easy, Red. We'll take care of you." He bent down and took her mouth again.

Wet, wonderful, she opened to him, received his tongue, their tango an erotic preview of the hot and heavy in-and-out movements she hoped would soon follow.

Cool air brushed her breasts as Henry lifted her T-shirt, pulled up her bra, and then closed his mouth over one nipple. He suckled her hard, and Tamara rocked her hips, back and forth in a raw plea. Male growls communicated feral desire, and she knew none of them had any doubt where this foreplay was headed.

"Oh, God." On the verge of a complete meltdown, Tamara shivered, so close to the edge she could only mew in need.

Morgan broke their kiss. "Here, now." He unsnapped her jeans, worked the zipper down, then slid his hand inside her pants, under her panties until he stroked her hot, wet cunt. Then he took her mouth again as he speared a finger inside her. He stroked her deeply, once, then added a second finger to torment her.

Tamara sucked his tongue, pressed her breast closer to Henry's mouth, and rode Morgan's fingers hard and fast. Her orgasm exploded, a deep, pulsing pleasure so wonderful, so heady, she wanted it never to end.

Masculine murmurs of encouragement cushioned her as she soared and soared, as her body shivered and her skin quivered and her pussy gushed into Morgan's hand.

As if they knew her body completely, the men ended their ministrations as she came down, as the ecstasy ebbed, and she was left with a pounding heart and sated senses.

"I've never…" She couldn't finish the sentence. She wasn't even standing on her own. Morgan's arm had come around her waist, and she knew if it hadn't, she'd have fallen on her ass on the floor.

"Never what, sweetheart?" Morgan placed a gentle kiss on her forehead.

"You've never come? Or come so fast?" Henry's fingers brushed her nipple lightly, and then he pulled her bra down to cover her and eased her T-shirt back into place.

Tamara opened her mouth to answer, but another voice, sultry and feminine, floated up the stairs.

"Morgan? Henry? Are you up there?"

"Oh, God!" Tamara felt the snap back to reality like a slap across the face.

"Shh," Henry whispered as he, too, placed a kiss on her forehead.

"We'll be right down, Mother," Morgan said.

"Your *mother* is here?"

A masculine voice said, "We'll wait in the kitchen. Make some coffee."

"Good idea, Charles," another masculine voice said. "I brought over some of Taylor's scones earlier, and I do believe there's enough to go around."

"So that's where they went," a third voice said. "And here I thought my faculties were failing me."

The sound of retreating footsteps reached her, and she looked at first Henry and then Morgan. "Sounds like your mother brought some friends with her." The voices and everyday conversation finished the job of pulling Tamara out of her lassitude. She took a step away from Henry.

Morgan turned her and reached down, raising her zipper and fastening her pants. She shook her head, not certain why she'd just stood there and let him fix her clothing as if she were a two-year-old.

"Friends?" He bent down and kissed her, a fast, fleeting touch of his lips on hers that despite her recent orgasm tasted like more.

"You could say she brought some friends with her," Henry agreed. "Three friends, in fact. Our fathers."

Tamara blinked. "You have three fathers? How is that even possible?"

Morgan's chuckle, intimate and deep, caressed her like a firm, warm hand.

"It's possible because, Red, that's how Kendalls do things. Come on, Dad's scones are *not* to be missed."

Tamara let Morgan take her hand and lead her toward the stairs. The smart-ass inside her wouldn't be silent.

I started the day with a plane crash...and then *everything just got weird from there.*

Chapter 5

"Ah, there you are. You must be Tamara. I'm so pleased to meet you."

Tamara couldn't help but gawk at the beautiful red-haired, green-eyed woman who came over to her, smile wide, arms outstretched. Before she could take even a breath, those arms enfolded her in a hug that, for reasons she didn't want to think about just then, made her want to cling, and maybe cry just a little. The woman was taller than her, of course, and the urge to lay her head on her breast and burrow in shocked her.

Tamara usually didn't like other women—not easily, and especially not on first meeting. But she found herself instantly liking Mrs. Kendall.

"Itty, this is our mother, Samantha, and our fathers, Charles, Preston, and Taylor." Each man raised his hand in turn, but Tamara didn't know if she could keep their names straight. She felt more than a little emotionally off balance.

Henry came to stand beside her, his smile wide and cocky—the way she'd gotten used to seeing it.

"*Itty?*" Samantha raised one eyebrow, and her gaze narrowed as she looked at her son.

Tamara wanted to laugh when Henry's cheeks turned a light pink and his expression became sheepish. "Um, for 'Itty-bitty,' on account of, well, she is."

Samantha's eyes widened. She shot an equally parental look at Morgan. "Is that what *you* call Tamara, too?"

"No, ma'am, of course not. I call her *Red*."

One of their fathers—she had no idea which one—snickered. Apparently Samantha had no trouble knowing which one, for she looked over her shoulder and said, "Taylor, please stop laughing and pour Tamara a cup of coffee."

"Of course, my love. Ms. Jones, why don't you come and join us men at the table, here," Taylor said.

"Good call, Taylor. Keep her out of the line of fire, as it were." His eyes sparkled with humor. "I'm Preston, by the way. Don't worry if you can't sort us out on first meet."

"You can call us each Dad, and then that way at least one of us is sure to answer."

Tamara deduced it was Charles who said that.

"I likely *won't* be able to keep you straight. You all look somewhat alike."

"Indeed we do," Taylor said. "That's because we're triplets. Fraternal, not identical, at least not on the outside." He set a cup of coffee down in front of her. Preston passed her the cream, Charles the sugar.

She looked over at Morgan and Henry, surprised to find they hadn't moved, but waited silently, bravely bearing their mother's stare, and standing at parade rest. Samantha Kendall stood before them, her arms crossed in front of her chest as if she was trying to decide which one had sinned the most and therefore deserved the greater punishment.

"Did they at least ask you if you were all right after your harrowing experience this morning, Tamara?" Samantha looked over at her.

It was too good an opportunity to pass up. She hadn't been able to gain the upper hand with these two flyboys since she'd met them. So she grinned and ratted them out. "No, ma'am. That one," she pointed to Morgan, "hit me with a running tackle, threw me to the ground, and pinned me there. And then that one," she pointed to Henry, "held me off the ground like I was a squirming puppy and didn't put me down for the *longest* time."

"More like a spitting kitten," Henry said. "And I was *trying* to avoid your wildly kicking feet, *Itty*."

Samantha closed her eyes and slowly shook her head. "I would wish the two of you all sons, but I have a feeling that would just punish your wife. Therefore, may you have half a dozen daughters to drive you to total distraction."

"Ouch," Preston said.

"Can you imagine if we'd had all girls instead of all boys?" Charles asked.

"No, I can't." Taylor shuddered. "Nor do I want to. No offense to the ladies among us."

"Sons." Samantha's pronouncement made both Morgan and Henry cringe.

"Sorry, Mother." Morgan leaned over and kissed her right cheek. "We'll try to do better."

"Sorry, Mother." Henry kissed her left one. "We really will."

Samantha hugged each one in turn. "Don't try. *Do*." Then she came over and placed a hand on Tamara's shoulder. "*Are* you all right after your harrowing ordeal this morning?"

Tamara couldn't help but smile. "I'm fine, really. And in their defense, they were trying to get me away from the plane until they were certain it wouldn't explode. If I had been thinking clearly, I'd have stepped well away from the Piper as soon as I was out of it for the same reason."

"You managed to land a single-engine plane without benefit of a working engine," Preston said.

"That was clear thinking enough," Charles said. He got up and gave his wife his chair, while Taylor set a cup of coffee in front of her.

"I understand Terry is going to lend his expertise at fixing it," Charles said. "He's a damn fine airplane mechanic."

"The man could easily get a job at any of the major airlines and pull in six figures a year," Taylor said. "Instead, he serves his country as an Air Force Chief Master Sergeant."

"I'd almost forgotten that he's coming home for Susan's ceremony on Saturday," Samantha said. "It will be good to see him again."

"He's taking two weeks' leave," Morgan said.

"Oh, then your plane couldn't have come down at a better time." Charles blinked. "Oh, dear, that didn't come out quite right at all, did it? What I meant was, Terry gets restless after a few days away from the flight line. He likes to have his hands in an engine."

"First he haunts the airfield," Taylor said. "Then he's raising the hoods of all our cars."

"Like I told you," Morgan said as he sat down beside her, "our cousin likes to keep busy."

"You've all been very kind to me. I don't want to—"

"You're not imposing," all three senior Kendall males interrupted her and answered at once.

Tamara looked from them to Samantha.

"I believe that was my line when I first came to Lusty so many years ago. Only instead of a broken-down airplane, I had a broken-down car."

"And not a penny in your pocket, if I recall," Preston said.

"Well, I have money, so—"

"So you can keep that in *your* pocket. We already told you, accepting payment for hospitality is not how Kendalls do things." Morgan sounded as if he absolutely would not be defied on the matter. "You can give us a hand at the building site, instead, if you feel you must 'pay' for our help. Money we have. Help with the construction, not so much."

Instead of acknowledging his decree, she turned her attention to his mother. "The males in your family bear more than a passing resemblance to bulldozers," she said.

Samantha laughed. "Yes, they do. It's how Kendalls do things."

Tamara was beginning to believe that single tagline covered a multitude of sins.

* * * *

Peter Alvarez parked his aging Ford Crown Victoria in an open spot directly in front of the Lusty Historical Society Museum. He rotated his shoulders, trying to work the kinks out from the long hours spent behind the wheel over the last couple of days. His stomach rumbled, reminding him he'd missed lunch. His watch read three-thirty. He'd passed a restaurant just down the street, but the sign on the museum stated the hours were Monday to Friday, 10:00 a.m. to 4:00 p.m.

Knowledge before food. The story of my life. No signs prohibited parking, and no meters stood ready to eat his change. He liked Lusty, Texas, already. It had always been his plan to come here someday, ever since he'd heard his *abuela* speak of the unique little town and the people who lived here when he'd been a teen.

His grandmother had never been able to decide if she was scandalized or awed by the place. Peter could appreciate her conflict. It had been the Catholic in her warring with compassion for the immigrants her own grandparents had been.

Peter didn't bother to lock his car. Instead, he just left it and entered the museum. Again, he could see no box asking for donations, or any sign that one couldn't simply just wander around at will.

He raised one eyebrow at the third large photograph on the wall just inside the door. The picture had been enlarged, likely with the aid of a computer program. The quality of the print was good. The sepia color, so universal in the photographs of the late nineteenth century, did nothing to detract from the mood of the picture. The photo captured six people, everyone smiling, as if sharing a good joke.

What struck him about the photograph the most—aside from the smiling faces, so *not* de rigueur of the day—was that the people in it had been posed as if it was just another family portrait.

He read the inscription, although he'd immediately recognized three of the subjects pictured. He had seen photos of them in one of Abuela's old albums.

"Why, hello there, young man."

Peter turned at the sound of the voice. A middle-aged woman with white-blond hair swept up in a neat bun atop her head, a sweet smile, and twinkling eyes made her way over to stand beside him.

"We don't get many strangers in here, but welcome. I'm Anna Jessop, the curator of the museum."

Something about the woman made Peter want to grin. She barely reached his shoulder and put him in mind of Mrs. Santa Claus—or his *tia abuela* Rosita.

"It's nice to meet you, Mrs. Jessop." He gave in to the urge and smiled. "I'm Peter Alvarez. I've been meaning to make this pilgrimage for years, but kept putting it off. And then I had to travel to Waco this week and thought, it's not that much farther to Lusty, so here I am."

"What on earth would make a Virginian want to make a pilgrimage to Lusty, Texas? We're not a very large town."

How does she know where I'm from? Before he could ask that out loud, she gave him a grin and waved her hand in a dismissive gesture.

"Sorry. I've got a good ear for accents. I don't detect much of the Hispanic in yours, despite your last name, if you don't mind my saying."

Peter liked to stick as close to the truth as humanly possible. It made the lies easier to support.

"No, I don't mind, and you wouldn't. My father is fourth generation American, and has no accent, either. The first generation of our family settled in this area back in 1870, or thereabouts." He pointed to the picture. "That's them there—Rita and José Mendez, and José's sister, Rosa. Family lore has it that they started out working for a man as mean as he was rich by the name of Tyrone Maddox. And then one day God answered their prayers of deliverance and brought them a new mistress by the name of Sarah Carmichael Maddox, who, after her husband's death, married a man—or two—named Benedict."

"Well, I'll be! You're not a stranger, then, at all. Did you know you have kin here? Some of the Mendez's grandchildren and great-grandchildren married into the Benedict and Jessop branches of the family. Then, of course there's the Sanchez family, over on Warren Drive. They're descendants of Rita and José, too."

Peter knew his shock showed. "No one told me that! I had no idea there'd be family still in the area."

"We take special care, here in Lusty, recording our genealogies and family trees. If you come back another day when I've more time, I'll get the old journals out for you to peruse."

"Thanks, I'd like that." Since he'd hoped to stay in the area until things broke, it sounded like an item to go on his "to do" list, something to give him a reason to stay around longer.

"Are you staying at one of the motels out by the highway?" Mrs. Jessop asked.

"Yes, I am. I'm at the Mesquite Lodge."

"Well, good then. Maybe you can come back tomorrow if you don't have to rush off."

"Actually, I'm kind of footloose at the moment. My job got downsized last month."

"Oh, my, that is a shame! And it's happening everywhere! Well, we close up here in just a few minutes. I'd give you longer, but I'm expected home, and I like to be on time. You're welcome to spend the time remaining looking around. It was so nice to meet you, Mr. Alvarez."

"Nice to meet you, too, Mrs. Jessop."

The woman trundled off, and Peter was left with the sensation of having been grilled by a professional interviewer. He knew of a few government agencies that could do worse than to hire Anna Jessop.

Peter made a mental note to hold his cards a little closer to the vest and be wary of spritely middle-aged women.

He duly walked the rest of the aisle he was in, looking at the pictures, reading the captions. He saw Benedicts and Kendalls and Jessops. He saw Parkers and Joneses and Parker-Joneses. Holy hell, he saw Bat Masterson and Wyatt Earp! No doubt those were actually the western legends looking relaxed and among friends as he'd taken history in college and was familiar with their images.

Peter kept an eye on the time, and when it was just a few minutes to closing, he waved at Mrs. Jessop and left the museum.

His instincts were alive and well. He stretched, looking up and down Main Street. Then he directed his feet toward the restaurant, just a block and a bit away that he'd passed earlier.

"*Lusty Appetites*. Cute name."

Peter opened the door and stepped into a whole lot of very tempting aromas. His stomach rumbled again, louder this time, and just as a red-haired waitress approached.

"Sounds like you got here just in time. Are you expecting someone to join you?"

"No, I'm solo."

"Then right this way." She led him to a table for two in the front corner of the restaurant beside the plate glass window.

"Perfect," he said. He took a seat facing the door and gave the waitress his best smile.

"I'm Carla, and I'll be serving you today. Our dinner special is available as of 4:00 p.m., and it's spicy pulled pork with Tex-Mex rice and your choice of green beans or fried okra. The special also includes your choice of a mixed greens salad, or slaw, and a piece of pie for dessert."

She had handed him the menu, but he gave it right back to her. "I like the sound of your special. I'll have that, with green beans and the mixed greens salad, with honey mustard dressing if you have it."

"We do. Would you care for something to drink?"

"Is your coffee fresh?"

"Yes, sir, I just made it a few minutes ago myself."

"Then I'll have some of that, thank you."

"I'll be right back with your coffee."

Peter relaxed in the comfortable chair and let his mind wander. He'd been on the go nonstop since early yesterday morning. As it looked like he might be in the area for a few days, at least, maybe he would get some time to decompress.

The door to the restaurant opened, and Peter's attention was snagged by the appearance of the khaki-brown uniform with a badge pinned to the front of it. The man looked ripcord lean. His gaze narrowed as he scanned the dining room. Then his gaze landed on Peter, and he directed his steps toward him.

Despite the fact that he'd obviously come to the restaurant specifically to see him, Peter had the feeling he hadn't been the first person the lawman had looked for.

"Afternoon. You're new in town, aren't you?" The sheriff's expression seemed friendly enough. But Peter saw the intelligence in his eyes. *Here is a man one should never underestimate.*

"I am. Been meaning to come here since I was a boy. But I imagine Mrs. Jessop told you all that, already."

"She did."

Adam pulled out the chair opposite him and sat. Just then the waitress came over with two cups of coffee. She set one in front of the sheriff, serving him first. Her smile, apologetic, eased the sting some. She left without saying a word.

"You'll have to excuse our caution," the sheriff said. "Six months ago a stranger came to town and ended up damn near killing one of our women."

"I hope you caught the bastard." Peter was a twenty-first century man, but nothing irked him more than men who victimized women.

"Yep, we did. *And* we learned a hard lesson."

"So you question every stranger who comes to town?"

"Nope. Just the ones who seem lean, mean, and dangerous to know." The sheriff did smile then, just a little. "Those were Aunt Anna's words, exactly. I'm afraid Kelsey's near miss frightened her very badly."

Yes, the feds really are missing a fantastic resource in Anna Jessop. Peter smiled, because in spite of everything, he actually felt complimented.

"I laud your caution, Sheriff..."

"Adam Kendall."

"You're named for one of the town's founders." Peter narrowed his gaze as if having to search for the detail. "That Adam Kendall was a lawman, too. A Texas Ranger, if I'm not mistaken."

"He was." The sheriff took a sip of his coffee then sat back. "Being law officers is the only thing we have in common, he and I."

Peter gave high marks to the man's perception. "That's too bad. Well, like I said, I laud your caution. So go ahead and ask me anything you like. My life is an open book."

Peter remained relaxed in a situation he knew would make a lot of men nervous. He could keep his story straight and would even insist on giving Adam his driver's license so the man could "run him."

Nothing untoward would come back, of course. Peter's bosses had worked long and hard to make sure his cover ran deep.

Chapter 6

Tamara hadn't known family dinners could be like this.

She wasn't exactly certain how it happened, but somehow she wound up having dinner with the entire Kendall family. The meal proved delicious, noisy, organized, and *fun*.

"I wanted to drive by that hangar y'all are supposed to be building," Jake, one of Morgan and Henry's brothers, said. "Nearly drove past it, it's so..." He looked right at Tamara and said, "itty-bitty."

Henry grinned, and Morgan looked down at his plate. Tamara could only laugh.

"Don't you worry, brother," Jordan said. "We're going to take up a collection and buy you a pair of glasses, so you can see better. Just as soon as we find someone who can make a pair that'll fit over that big honking nose of yours."

A man appeared at the door of the dining room, wearing a khaki-brown uniform and an apologetic expression. "Sorry I'm late, Mother. Hey, Jordan. Good to have you home, brother."

"Adam! I was beginning to worry," Samantha said. She got up and gave him a hug, just the same as she'd done when Jordan had come in a few minutes before.

Tamara had expected that hug because Morgan had explained that Jordan had been gone for several weeks, tied up in negotiations for his construction company. Adam, however, lived in Lusty, so Samantha likely saw him every day. "Sit down, sweetheart, and dig in. This is Tamara Jones, no relation that we can figure to the Lusty Joneses."

"Oh, I wouldn't say she isn't—" Henry's drawl drew Tamara's glare and his mother's immediate censure.

"Henry!"

"Yes, ma'am."

"Ah, the *little lady* who crash-landed on the airstrip this morning," Adam said as he sat down.

Samantha turned to her. "When they were *children*, they would all harass and tease each other and guests unmercifully," she said sweetly.

"You mean, kind of like the way they're doing now?" Tamara asked.

"Exactly!" Samantha smiled.

"Uh-oh. Our Tamara is a sharp cookie," Taylor said to his sons. "You best watch yourselves. You'll be sliced and diced in no time."

Tamara's mouth opened at being referred to as theirs.

"So why *are* you late, lawman?" Morgan asked Adam. "Sudden crime wave hit Lusty?"

"Aunt Anna called, concerned about a stranger who came into the museum just before it closed."

"That poor woman!" Samantha said. "She still hasn't gotten over what happened to Kelsey last summer. I'll rearrange my schedule and spend some time with her." Samantha looked up at Adam. "Did she have any cause to be concerned?"

"Not as far as I have been able to determine. Man's name is Peter Alvarez. Actually, he's descended from the original Mendez family. He checks out fine. He's just a man who found himself out of a job and who decided to look up his roots, far as I can tell."

"Oh yeah? Old? Young?" Jordan asked.

"He's thirty-five. Why?"

"Well, if he's going to be hanging around town for a while, maybe he'd like to earn a few bucks. I was planning to hire someone to give us a hand with the build." Then Jordan flashed Tamara a look of mock deference. "Not that I don't think you'll be a *really big* help."

Tamara snorted then flexed her nonexistent left bicep. She couldn't fully explain the emotions that had been running through her the last half hour or so, but she felt happy and amused.

The men exchanged a look that nearly had her giggling.

"I'll give you his hotel and room number after dinner," Adam said to his brother.

"Eat, boys," Samantha said.

"Yes, ma'am," the men chorused as one.

Tamara had to admire the way Samantha Kendall managed her family. It took a woman of superior intelligence and strength to keep eight men in line, in her opinion.

"Morgan, did you invite Tamara to Susan's wedding on Saturday?" Samantha asked.

"Not yet, Mother, but I plan to," Morgan said. He turned his gaze to her. "Susan is Susan Benedict, one of our cousins."

"I'm sure she wouldn't appreciate a perfect stranger coming to her wedding," Tamara said.

"You're pretty darn good, but I wouldn't necessarily say you're perfect," Henry said. "After all, you're itty—"

"Don't say it."

Tamara grinned at Samantha because they'd both spoken at the same time.

"And actually, Susan, Colt, and Ryder would be delighted for you to attend," Morgan said.

"Colt and Ryder. Those would be the bridegrooms?"

"See?" Morgan said. "Only one day with us, and you're not confused at all."

"No," Tamara said. She met his gaze, and then Henry's. "I think I'm finally figuring things out."

As an answer to a proposition, it wasn't the most poetic of sentences she could have come up with. But considering she'd delivered it in front of what could only be called a small crowd,

Tamara thought she'd gotten the message across in as private a manner as possible.

* * * *

Tamara eased the Cadillac CTS-V Coupe into the laneway, bringing it to a gradual stop. She sighed with relief and turned off the engine. Not usually a white-knuckle driver, she nonetheless had been the entire short trip from the Kendall's home—what they called the New House even though it was actually over a century old—to the *cottage* where she would be staying for the next while.

She pulled the keys from the ignition. Just before she opened the door, she closed her eyes and inhaled deeply. The car still smelled new, for crying out loud.

The door opened, and Tamara looked up. Morgan and Henry had followed her over in their Jeep. Henry held the door for her, with his brother close beside him.

"What kind of a person gives the keys of her *brand-new* Cadillac to a woman who that very morning crash-landed a plane?" she asked them.

"You didn't crash it," Henry said without missing a beat, "you successfully executed an emergency landing."

Tamara laughed so hard she had no strength to resist when Morgan pulled her out of the car and into his arms for a quick hug.

"What did Mother say to you when she gave you her keys?" Morgan laced the fingers of his left hand with her right. "Neither of us could make out her words."

"She said she didn't like the idea that I didn't have any options. She didn't want me to feel stuck in town—or with the two of you." Tamara smiled. "I really like your mother."

"That's a bonus," Henry took her other hand, "as we happen to really like her, too. *Most* of the time."

Tamara walked with them up the path to the porch. Looking up, she smiled at the fan some Kendall had thought to install—outside, on the ceiling of the porch—likely because Mother Nature had failed to cooperate sufficiently during one particular summer.

"You noticed that this afternoon, too," Henry said.

"I think it's quaint."

"The air can be stifling sometimes in the summer. Of course, now we have air-conditioning installed here. A few decades ago, they only had fans in the house, and nothing outside." Morgan held out his hand for the key. Tamara gave it to him. He unlocked and then held the door open for her, and she realized she felt a little miffed having to relinquish his hand in order to go inside.

They'd left a single light burning in the short entrance hallway, and one at the top of the stairs.

Henry closed the door behind him, shutting the three of them inside, together. He moved subtly then, so that she was between them.

The air felt heavy with sexual tension, and a delicious heat curled in her stomach, sending out tiny tendrils of fire to lick her nerve endings.

"It's been an eventful day for you." Morgan's voice, low, sexy, made her nipples hard. She clenched her inner muscles in response to the shiver that centered on her clit.

"Do you want to know what happens next?" His voice continued to caress and tease her senses.

Tamara smiled. Even after hours and a wonderful meal, his taste from that afternoon was still on her lips. Henry's heat and essence also lingered on her tongue.

They'd given her the best orgasm she'd had in years. She wanted more of their heat.

"I think I have a very good idea what happens next." She couldn't stand it that they weren't touching her anymore. One step brought her to Morgan.

His slow, sexy smile lit some more of her kindling. At this rate, she'd go up in flames in no time.

"Let's see if you're right." He leaned down and brushed her lips with his, back and forth, a gentle caress that renewed the heat they'd shared earlier.

Tamara mewed. Deep inside her, hunger for these two Kendalls burned. She wanted more. She wanted it all.

"Shh." The sound vibrated against her lips. He slid an arm around her waist and drew her against him so they stood flush. The press of his rigid cock against her stomach thrilled her and assured her he wanted just as much, burned just as hot, as she.

Yet his lips continued a light glide and slide, a moist and subtle wooing. She'd never been wooed, never been seduced, and despite the impatience gnawing at her, she found she liked this slow and easy pace.

"You taste good, Red. Hot and sassy, wild and exotic. I could drink you for hours."

"Please." She longed for him to sink into her. She wanted to absorb his scent, his heat.

"Open for me, then, baby. Let me plunder."

Tamara opened her mouth with no thought of denial, seeking only to surrender, to plunge into the abyss of mindless arousal. Wet and wonderful, his mouth suckled hers, and his tongue penetrated her mouth with broad, bold strokes. Again and again he surged into her, tasting, drinking, and devouring all she offered, giving so much in return.

When his lips left hers, she whimpered. Morgan stroked her bottom lip with one finger, then nudged her toward his brother.

"Do you have any idea how incredibly hot you make us, melting for us like that?" Henry's words kissed her cheeks, her nose, and her eyes.

"Kiss me."

"Ah, Itty-Bitty, I want to gulp you right down."

His mouth captured hers, his taste as potent, his command of her as deep and as total as his brother's. Elemental, raw, his tongue tangled with hers, dancing, seducing her completely. Shivers wracked her, arousal shimmered through her, fed by the taste of this man, the heat of him and his brother, and the sultry promise of earthy, feral sex.

Then she blinked as Henry ended their kiss and stepped back. Before she could think, Morgan turned her into his arms and picked her up as if she was no more than that puppy she'd likened herself to earlier.

"Hang on to me, Red. It's bedtime."

She clung to him, arms and legs a human clamp, not allowing herself to think too deeply that she had never been a woman to cling. He mounted the steps with her, each footfall in cadence with her pounding, excited heart.

He set her down beside the bed and captured her lips once more. This kiss differed from the last, less masterful, more coaxing. She felt the rub of his hands up and down her back, kneading, cupping, and pressing her against his cock. It felt hotter and harder than before, and Tamara rolled her hips, trying to caress it. She could feel the lips of her cunt thickening as if they could capture him. The sound that emerged from her throat spoke eloquently of edgy desire.

"When I get inside you, you're going to burn, sweetheart." Morgan kissed the words along the curve of her jaw.

"I'm burning now. Please. I need you. Oh, God, I need you both."

"Hush, sweet baby." Henry wrapped his arms around her from behind and nuzzled her. His tongue lapped, his lips kissed, caressing the shell of her ear and the column of her neck, and she shivered with horniness. His hands stroked up and down over her breasts, and she moaned and arched her back, pushing her greedy nipples closer to his wonderful touch.

"We want to see you, touch you. Will you let us?" Morgan had been watching her with his brother, and the arousal in his eyes was almost palpable.

They meant to share her, and for the first time she realized how doing so would very much pleasure *them*, as well as her. There appeared to be no jealousy between them at all.

To have two mouths, two cocks, focused on her would be every woman's fantasy made real. To have *their* mouths, *their* cocks, would be a thrill beyond her wildest imagining.

"Yes, yes, anything. Everything."

Henry slid his hands down to the edge of her T-shirt, then under. Morgan took the edge of it and began to lift it. "Arms up, sweetheart."

Tamara raised her arms, and the garment sailed up and off. Morgan dropped it on the floor then used a single finger to trace, back and forth, over the tops of her breasts above her bra.

"Your skin is so soft and silky, here."

Henry brought one hand to her back. His fingers easily unhooked the clasp. That same hand brushed first her right strap down, and then the left.

Morgan pulled the lacy bit of lingerie from her and dropped it on top of her shirt.

"I wondered what color your nipples would be. Would they be darkly brown, or lushly pink? Look at them, so sweet and peachy and responsive." He used just a finger to circle and tease, turning them pebble hard. "Do they taste like peaches, I wonder?"

Before she could form a word he bent and suckled her. Oh, God, the pull of his mouth, so hot and strong, touched off tiny explosions of excitement in her clit.

Henry cupped her other breast, tweaking and pulling that nipple between thumb and forefinger.

"I wonder if we could make you come just by playing with your breasts?"

"I don't...I've never..." She tried to tell them she'd never received much pleasure from having her breasts played with, but the words tangled in her throat.

"That's because you weren't under our hands, Tamara." Morgan's arrogant statement rang of truth.

In response, Tamara could only moan and roll her hips, a wordless plea for more.

Morgan glanced at Henry. "Let me hold her. It's your turn."

The words made no sense until Henry turned her so that Morgan held her from behind. Henry unsnapped, unzipped, and then pulled her jeans and panties down her legs and off.

She stood totally naked, held by one man while another rubbed his hand, back and forth, over her slit. She felt cream from her pussy leaking onto Henry's hand. He grunted, deep and low, and she knew he liked that.

"Mm, so wet. So hot. So close. Let's see what we can do about that."

It felt like the afternoon all over again as broad, long male fingers penetrated her body, sliding into her cunt to stroke, reaching deep. Henry finger-fucked her, slow, sure thrusts that burned, that thrilled, that had her nearly begging to come. She shook as her climax neared, as it danced close then retreated.

Morgan shifted his hold on her and nuzzled her ear. Then he sucked his own finger into his mouth, wetting it, then pulled it out.

And rubbed that finger back and forth over her anus.

"Oh, God!" She came with a flood of pleasure, a gush of rapture so great she actually screamed as her body shook with each pounding spasm. Fast and furious, flush and full, her orgasm filled her and emptied her and robbed her of every one of her senses. She came and came and came until she groaned for mercy.

Henry tilted her face and mated his lips to hers, the penetration of his tongue as carnal as the plundering of his fingers had been.

He lifted her and held her as she continued to shake, as the aftershocks battered her from within.

"Here." Morgan's voice, coming from farther away than he had been, roused her. Henry moved and swung her down and handed her over to Morgan.

Tamara gasped from the chill of the sheets as Morgan drew her against his hot, naked flesh.

When had he stripped and gotten into the bed? She didn't get a moment to think about it because in mere seconds, Henry lifted the sheets and slid into the bed on the other side of her.

"Go to sleep, Itty." He kissed her shoulder then pressed himself against her back.

"Sleep? But you…neither of you—"

"We can wait, Red. Contrary to recently voiced opinions, not every man needs to rut to find pleasure, or puts his own fulfillment before his woman's. You've had a hell of a day. You fell asleep in Henry's arms a few moments ago and didn't even realize it. Now you can fall asleep in mine."

"You're bossy."

"I am."

Tamara's heart warmed. This was a new experience, one she'd never imagined she'd have. And she appreciated it, more than she had words to say. But she wanted very badly to feel their cocks inside her.

She yawned, snuggling down, fully intending to rest just a moment before she wound them up and did some plundering of her own. She wanted to see how far and how fast they'd fly together.

That thought put a smile on her face even as she felt herself sinking into sleep.

Chapter 7

A lifetime spent in the military had imprinted several habits on Morgan Kendall. He'd only been a civilian for just under a month, so he wouldn't have expected any of those habits to have faded already.

One of the most irritating habits was awakening at an ungodly hour, every single morning. He turned his head to look at the bedside clock. 4:48 a.m. He hadn't slept past five in the morning in years. Hell, he wasn't just up with the chickens, he was up with the fucking worms.

A soft huff of air against his shoulder drew his gaze, and his attention, to his right. Beside him and snuggled in close, Tamara slept deeply. His mouth relaxed into a smile as he simply watched her. *Hell of a thing*.

Morgan had just learned that a person could be aware of familial traits and family history his entire life and still be pole-axed when what he'd assumed would someday happen to him actually happened.

His fathers had fallen in love with his mother at first sight. He'd asked each of them once how they knew it was love they'd felt and not just lust. Those brothers Kendall had each said almost the exact same thing—that there'd been a sense of connection the moment they'd laid eyes on the red-haired, green-eyed Samantha Kincaid. As if, they'd gone on to say, they'd known her all their lives and had been *waiting* for her, and waiting for the privilege of taking care of her.

As a sixteen-year-old know-it-all, Morgan figured his dads had just handed him a line of pure bullshit.

As a thirty-five-year-old man who'd met his future wife just yesterday, he finally got it.

It didn't matter that he and Henry had decided to get their business up and running and *then* begin to think about a mate, or that they'd figured that the latter half of their life plan wouldn't be happening for another couple of years yet.

Yesterday Tamara Jones had fallen out of the sky—*thank you very much, Kate Benedict*—and today both he and his brother knew what their future would be.

Tamara frowned in her sleep, reminding him of how fierce and stubborn she could be when riled. He'd certainly seen signs of that yesterday. So Morgan mentally tacked a "we hope" on to the end of that last mental assertion. He wondered how long it would take them to convince Tamara Jones that she belonged with them.

Morgan sensed he was being watched. Looking over to the far side of the bed, he met Henry's gaze. Henry glanced toward the bedroom door, then back at him. Morgan nodded in understanding. They both got out of the bed carefully, each tucking the blanket close around their woman so she'd stay asleep for awhile yet.

Morgan had been serious last night when he told Tamara she'd had a hell of a day yesterday. He knew at the time she hadn't understood that he and Henry both intended to see she rested well. That resolve hadn't changed. She needed her sleep now. They each snagged the pants they'd dropped on the floor the night before and then left the bedroom. Making their way downstairs in the dark, they both moved silently.

Morgan had been trained to move with stealth and make his way anywhere, anytime, undetected. Henry, he knew, came by the talent naturally.

"She was wiped last night," Henry said quietly once they'd entered the kitchen.

"Can't blame her. I had to dead stick a Cessna once. Sure as hell took the starch out of me for a good long while."

Henry grinned. "I've never had that experience. The planes I flew didn't offer that option, to be perfectly honest. If *those* aircraft fucked up, the pilot's only choice was to punch out. End of story."

"That's even worse," Morgan said. He set about brewing a pot of coffee. Outside the window, the deep black of night began to lighten to a pearl gray. Soon that gray would give way to a beautiful Texas dawn.

"What time is Jordan meeting us at the site this morning?"

"Nine. He was going to head on over to the IHOP over by the Interstate and meet with that guy Adam told us about at dinner last night," Morgan said.

"Since our brother the sheriff has already checked the man out, I say, hire him."

"It may or may not be that simple," Morgan said. When Henry raised one eyebrow, he explained, "Adam told me the man checked out, but he got some vibes from him that he couldn't completely explain."

"Well, Jordan will figure it out. He's got pretty good people sense, too."

They were dancing around the most important subject, and Morgan knew it.

"It's probably my fault," Henry said at last. "Mother always said one day I'd pay for having everything so easy all my life."

Morgan grinned. "So she did." Then he frowned. "I wasn't ready for her, either, that's for damn sure. But that doesn't make a difference. She's ours."

"That's how I feel, too. I kind of like her prickly side."

Morgan chuckled. "Me, too." Then he sobered. "I'll tell you one thing that's been bothering me, though."

"The fact that this Mr. John Smith from outside of Abilene allowed Tamara to take off in that plane without giving her any paperwork at all, not even a bill of sale," Henry said.

"Exactly." It didn't surprise him that he and his favorite brother were on the same page. "She said her uncle and Smith were old friends, so maybe it's all fine, and the man is sending the papers on to her uncle at a later date," Morgan said.

"And maybe we should ask Adam to run the registration on the Piper, just in case," Henry finished.

"It certainly couldn't hurt. I'm going to be pissed if it turns out either her uncle or that Smith character took advantage of Tamara's trusting nature."

"That makes two of us. I'll find a moment to give Adam a call when we get to the site," Henry said. "No need to let her know what we're doing. She'd only worry, and we don't want that."

"My feelings, exactly. The sooner we have an answer in that area, the better I'll like it," Morgan said. He knew things in the world could be twisted and convoluted and crooked as hell. Maybe it was his experience with the seamier elements in life, thanks to some of the work he'd undertaken for Uncle Sam, that had made him suspicious of the story Tamara had told him. Maybe it was instinct. Oh, he believed Tamara believed what she'd told them, completely. One look in those witchy-hazel eyes of hers and he saw the truth. "In the meantime, we take care of our woman the way Kendalls do."

"Bet your ass we do," Henry said.

"*Your* woman?"

Morgan turned toward the sound of the sleepy, feminine voice. *God in heaven she turns me on*. She stood there at the door to the kitchen, looking warm and bed-rumpled, her sassy, fiery brown hair nicely mussed. She'd grabbed his T-shirt and slipped it on over her head. On her it wore very nearly like a minidress, but he'd bet if she raised her arms over her head, he'd get a wonderful glimpse of pussy.

"Do you have a problem with that?" he asked her.

"Not so much a problem with it, as that I'm confused by it."

"I thought we cured your confusion yesterday," Henry said.

"You cured *that* confusion. This is a different confusion entirely."

Tamara looked from him to his brother, her brow drawn up as if she was trying, but not very hard, to contain her inner grump.

Morgan smiled. Damned if he didn't really like this side of her. He shot a glance at Henry, who was also smiling in a way that told Morgan he felt the same way.

Point of fact, he bet he knew what she claimed to be "confused" about. He was also of the opinion that she wasn't really confused. She was *pissed*.

"If you tell us what it is you're confused about, we'll be happy to un-confuse you." Morgan gave her his best smile.

"You didn't fuck me last night."

"No, ma'am, we didn't," Henry said, and Morgan could hear the suppressed laughter in his response.

"Not that we didn't want to." Morgan ambled over to her and raised her chin with his finger so that she could see the truth in his eyes. "If in the future you *ever* think to accuse us of being selfish lovers, remember this moment, and last night. We both went to sleep with raging hard-ons, and neither of us jerked off, either. We wanted you so bad our cocks *ached*."

"Now I *really* don't understand," Tamara said.

"You needed to know that we'll always put your needs—and your pleasure—above our own," Morgan said.

"The challenge you didn't mean to hand us yesterday," Henry reminded her.

"Well, hell."

She had such a pouty little face Morgan couldn't resist bending down and planting a kiss right on her luscious lips.

"I think you need some coffee, love," he said.

"If that's what you think I need, you weren't paying attention to my pout just now."

Morgan grinned. He looked over at his brother, met his gaze.

"Oh, we paid attention to it," Morgan said. "And we'd love nothing better than to take you right back to bed. But we've agreed to meet Jordan at the site by nine, which would only give us a couple of hours."

Henry stepped forward and ran his hand down Tamara's back. When she turned to look up at him, he gave her a very light kiss. "We can't love you properly in just a couple of hours. It's going to take us all night."

"And maybe all the next day, too," Morgan said. He kissed her again. "Now sit down, and we'll get you that coffee."

* * * *

The brothers Kendall were driving her crazy.

That was the only explanation Tamara had for her pouty-face, thoroughly frustrated mood. *Thank God they gave me a hammer and some nails.* Tamara stepped back from the piece of plywood she was working on and frowned. Those sneaky devils not only gave her a hammer and some nails, they set her to work in between them, but not so close to either of them that she would be tempted take out her frustration on them.

Tamara was beginning to think that those two flyboys were different from any men she'd ever known. They'd stripped her bare the night before and given her the best orgasm of her life, demonstrating that they somehow knew her body better than she did herself. And then they had tucked her in between them and told her to go to sleep.

It peeved her more than a little that she had done just that.

As she stood there staring at that stupid piece of wood, it occurred to her that what they'd done the night before had actually been the first time in her life that anyone had made her their focus and taken care of her. Not only had they taken care of her, but then this morning they'd more or less told her that what happened next was going to be entirely up to her.

The rats had put the ball firmly in her court. She'd have to make the next move. Tamara shook her head. In the course of just slightly more than twenty-four hours she'd gone from being shocked about the existence of a town called Lusty where ménage relationships seemed to be the norm, to trying to figure out the best where and when to try to grab such a relationship for herself.

Crap, it's not even just sex that I want. It's a complete, emotionally-involved relationship.

"Is something wrong?"

Tamara looked up. She hadn't heard Jordan Kendall approach. He was looking from her to the plywood and back. She knew she was scowling. She guessed she couldn't blame him for wondering.

"No, nothing's wrong," she said. "At least nothing here." She waved toward the wood. Point of fact, there were another five sheets Morgan and Henry had tacked in place that needed more than the few nails currently holding them in place.

Hell, her mind had been so messed up she hadn't even realized they'd given her busy work.

"I was coming over to see if you were ready to move on to a nail gun and some real work," he said quietly.

Tamara felt herself smile at the way Jordan had lowered his voice and seemed to be giving his brothers furtive glances as he said that. As if he didn't want them to overhear.

"I've never actually used a nail gun," she confided. "I've used a hammer often enough, though."

"Well, maybe there're some other jobs we can give you, then, when you've finished with your current assignment." He looked up at the sound of a car approaching. When the vehicle pulled into the parking area behind one of the hangars, Jordan mumbled something and moved off toward it.

The man who got out of the aging Ford was handsome in a Rodrigo Santoro kind of way. *Dark and dangerous, smooth and slick.* She tilted her head to one side as she watched him shift, accept

Jordan's handshake, while seeming to be taking in his surroundings. She had the impression the man was on alert, as if he expected an attack at any moment.

Tamara sensed she was no longer alone.

"Who's the beefcake?" she asked as Morgan and Henry moved to stand close beside her.

"What, you think he's good looking?" Henry stood on her left, moving closer to her even before he'd finished speaking.

"Well, I'm not blind, and he sure is pretty."

"Wasn't there some kind of old saying about pretty is as pretty does?" Morgan, on her right, shifted a bit closer, too.

Tamara thought it kind of cute the way Morgan and Henry got all protective of her because another, unknown male showed up.

She couldn't keep the smile off her face as she looked from one to the other of the flyboys.

"Are you two jealous?"

She turned her attention back to watching Jordan with the new arrival. As the two men spoke, they moved to the back of the Crown Vic. The driver opened the trunk and reached inside.

Moments later he pulled out a tool belt and began to put it on.

"Jealous? No, I wouldn't say we're jealous. Exactly." Morgan's voice came out kind of quiet. Tamara felt his eyes on her.

"No, not exactly," Henry agreed. "I'd say, 'cautious' is more in line with what we are."

"Yes," Morgan said. "Cautious."

Tamara giggled. Then she laid a hand on each man's back. "If I was any kind of a self-respecting female engaged in the male-slash-female tango, I'd let this go on and on. But, sadly, I never did care for playing games. So please allow me to put you out of your 'caution.'"

"You like us better," Henry said, and it sounded endearingly hopeful.

"Well, of course I do, but that wasn't what I was about to say. I was going to say that if anyone should be jealous, or cautious, it would be me. But whoever that man is, he hasn't noticed the two of you. He's got the hots for your brother."

She didn't know what kind of a reaction she'd expected, but the sighs of relief surprised her.

"That's probably what Adam was sensing," Henry said to Morgan.

"More than likely. I guess we should go over and introduce ourselves. Since we are Jordan's elder brothers, and all."

"Huh. I thought for certain you'd tell me I was imagining things," Tamara said.

"No, of course not," Henry said.

Morgan looked down at her. "We're just playing hell with all your preconceived notions about men, aren't we, Red?"

"Not so much preconceived as *learned* notions," Tamara said. "Experience is one hell of a great teacher."

"Clearly, you've encountered all the wrong kind of men in your life to date," Morgan said.

"There haven't been all that many men, flyboy, but I'm a fast learner."

"This gives me hope." Morgan bent down and gave her a kiss that was way too short.

"And you're really all right with Jordan being gay?"

"Remind us to share some of our family history with you sometime." Henry bent down and kissed her, too. "But in the meantime, and in the interest of accuracy, you should know that Jordan isn't gay. He's bisexual."

Before Tamara could comment on that, Morgan and Henry stepped away from her and headed toward their younger brother and the man who clearly had all of that man's attention.

Chapter 8

Henry left the airfield early, in order to have everything ready at the house for Tamara.

He stood back now as he took stock of all his preparations. He'd put fresh sheets on the bed and placed scented candles throughout the bedroom. Fresh water churned and heated in the Jacuzzi, and more candles gave that room a definite air of seduction. Supplies lined the shelf above the tub, and damned if he wasn't getting hard just thinking about using them on their woman.

An ice bucket with a bottle of champagne waited within easy reach of the spa, and another bottle chilled in the mini fridge in the bedroom.

Were they rushing her? Probably. Henry knew with absolute certainty that Tamara Jones was the woman he and Morgan had hoped to one day find, the woman destined to be theirs.

They'd found her—or she'd found them, earlier than they'd expected. Why should they wait?

Downstairs, Henry checked the slow cooker. He'd cheated there, having begged his mother's wonderful beef with mushrooms and wine. It would stay warm and ready for them until they were ready for it.

Both he and his brother knew how to cook and could prepare more than the standard man fare of outdoor grill or stir-fry. They'd lived on their own, on base and off, for a lot of years. Eating in restaurants got old very fast.

They would impress Tamara with their culinary expertise some other time. Tonight, they wanted all their efforts focused on impressing their woman in other, far more personal ways.

Henry checked his watch. He had another ten minutes until Morgan and Tamara came home from the construction site.

He set the dining room table and then made his way to the sound system. Tucked away in a corner of the parlor, it was wired to pipe music through the entire house. He queued up a number of jazz CDs and set the volume on low.

Something about the beat of jazz pulsing through the air reminded him of jungles and hot, steamy sex.

He and Morgan believed Tamara had never been properly romanced or seduced. They wanted to start out the way they meant to go. Every woman deserved the time and the effort to be wooed into the act of making love. And certainly no woman deserved that more than Tamara.

Of course it was far too soon to talk of futures, of weddings and family commitment ceremonies and children. Their tempestuous woman would likely run screaming in the opposite direction if she had any clue they were thinking of spending a lifetime with her at this early stage.

So for now they would woo her, and make love to her, and see if they couldn't crack that brick wall she'd built to protect her all too vulnerable heart.

Everything was ready, with one side benefit he hadn't expected. As he heard the sound of the Caddy pulling into the drive, a shiver of nerves jolted through him. He hadn't been nervous at the prospect of having sex with a woman since his first time, all those many years ago.

I'm nervous because Tamara matters.

Then she walked in the door, and Henry knew everything was going to be good.

"Wow, something smells delicious in here," Tamara said. She closed her eyes and inhaled deeply. Those actions made Henry's cock get even harder than it had been.

"Mm, the only thing I smell is you, and, sweetheart, delicious doesn't even begin to cover it." He stepped forward and cupped her face in his hands.

Tamara's eyes opened. He caught the startled flash and watched it give way to pleasure. Taking that look as all the permission he needed, Henry laid his mouth on hers.

He loved the taste of her, a mixture of sweet and tart that heated his blood and stirred his arousal. His cock sensed her nearness and stiffened even more. He slid his tongue into her mouth, pleased when hers stroked back, when the suction of her lips and the swirl of her tongue turned hot and avid.

Henry raised his head. The heat of her body pulsed a unique fragrance he found very erotic. "Tonight, we won't just make you come and tuck you into bed. Tonight, we plan to have you." He looked up and his gaze met Morgan's glittering one.

He caressed his hands from Tamara's cheeks to her shoulders then gently turned her to face his brother.

Morgan drew her closer. "Do you want us both, Tamara? Will you take us both into your body?"

No question, if she said no they'd back off. Of course they'd try again. And again. Kendalls always stopped at the word "no," but they didn't give up easily.

Tamara shivered. She reached up and stroked Morgan's face, and then glanced over her shoulder and met Henry's gaze.

"I had planned to give you a bit of time last night, and then I was going to pounce on you. Instead, I fell asleep. I woke up hungry for you, and that hunger has stayed with me all day. So, yes. Yes, I want you both."

He saw it then, the unspoken message that she'd take them for as long as their ardor lasted and consider it all just sex. Considering what she'd said about her parents, he could hardly blame her for believing that passion didn't last.

That was all right. As long as she was with them, as long as she was open to them, they had hope. All they needed was time to prove to her that passion did indeed last.

As long as she stayed there in Lusty, they had that time to prove to her that sometimes, passion became love and lasted forever.

* * * *

Before impending nerves and vulnerability had a chance to overwhelm her, Morgan lifted her into his arms.

"Wrap yourself around me, sweetheart."

His heat became hers as, with arms and legs, Tamara clamped onto him. He carried her, much as he had the night before. Since he was doing the walking for both of them, she felt free to do something else. She nuzzled her face against his neck and began to lick him.

Morgan's indrawn breath hissed between his teeth. "Easy, Red. I need a shower, first."

"I like the taste of you as you are, all work-sweaty and delicious."

"Lord, woman."

Since his heat increased and his step faltered, she guessed he liked what she'd said and what she was doing to him.

He hadn't even finished lowering her feet to the floor in the bathroom when he bent down and captured her mouth with his. He didn't kiss her, he devoured her. A secret part of her melted, eager to submit, to give everything without hesitation. And while this new urge felt exciting, it wasn't comfortable, and certainly had never been *her* before.

Tamara had always had trouble really letting go with a man.

Henry pressed against her back and ran his hands from her shoulders, down her arms, until he had her hands in his.

She slid her lips from Morgan's and tilted her head back. "I want to taste your sweat, too," she whispered to him.

"Good God, woman, you get me hot."

Morgan turned her around, and when Henry reached for her she jumped him, making him hold her, making him wrap his arms around her. She set her mouth on him, kissing, licking, and sucking his flesh.

"Mm, different, but just as tasty. Why do you two taste so damn good to me?"

"Careful, Itty, or you're going to be tasting us in a whole other way."

She grinned at the tight sound of Henry's voice. He set her down gently, and she stroked her hand over the erection that threatened to explode out of his jeans. "I want to suck your cocks. I want to suck both of them."

"Damn, Red, we're trying to give you a bit of romance, here." Morgan's half-laugh sounded stressed.

She reached out and stroked her hand over his cock, too. "I don't need romance. I don't *want* romance. I want to fuck you. Both of you."

She didn't know what kind of telepathy they had going between them, and couldn't really read the facial expressions that came, and then went, so quickly.

Morgan cupped her face, and when she met his gaze, the heat and the emotion she read there brought a lump to her throat.

"We beg to differ, Tamara Jones. Maybe you don't want romance. And maybe you simply don't know how much hotter, and yes, how much sweeter, the romance will make the sex. So why not let us have our way in this and see what you think afterwards?"

Tamara shivered. Something in his manner felt almost threatening, but she didn't know what or how or why. She did know she'd never been so turned on, never needed to be touched and stroked and fucked the way she needed all those things right now. She wanted to rush to the prize, and clearly, they weren't going to let her do that.

If putting up with a bit of romance was the price she had to pay to have her need for hot, sweaty jungle sex met, then so be it.

She had a feeling these two flyboys would meet her needs beyond her wildest expectations.

It took a lot of effort to get out of the driver's seat. "All right. Romance away."

She smelled it then, a soft, alluring fragrance. She turned her head as Henry came back to them. She hadn't noticed him stepping away. Neither had she realized he'd lit candles.

There had to be a dozen of them in small glass bowls, scattered throughout the room.

Henry put his hands gently on her shoulders, and Tamara started, just a little. Morgan gave her a slow, sexy smile.

"You know, Red, a woman who manages to dead-stick a plane as if she did it every day shouldn't be afraid of a little romance."

"I understand planes. Romance scares the hell out me." What was it about these two men that made her say things she'd normally keep to herself?

"It won't hurt you, sweetheart." Morgan lifted the hem of her T-shirt.

Tamara raised her arms, shivering when the cotton swept clear of her body. She felt Henry behind her, close and warm. Then his fingers stroked her back lightly just above the clasp of her bra before unfastening the small hooks.

Morgan gently pulled the lacy garment from her and dropped it to the floor.

Her nipples had peaked, and he took a moment to caress the underside of her breasts back and forth with the back of his hand.

Tamara sucked in a tiny breath. Morgan's gentle touch spiked her arousal. Her nipples drew up so tight they felt pinched, and that just drove her excitement higher, too.

"You're so incredibly sensitive, here," Morgan said.

"I never have been." They wanted to give her romance, to seduce her slowly when all she wanted was to have them on her and in her. She wanted to give them something in return. She wanted to give them the truth. "Having my breasts played with has never really turned me on before. The prospect of sex has never been this thrilling before."

"Ah, darling." Henry slipped his arms around her from behind. "That's probably because no one's ever taken the time to *learn* you."

"Before we close our eyes tonight, we're going to know you inside out," Morgan said.

Henry unsnapped her jeans and lowered the zipper. Morgan leaned down and suckled her right nipple into his mouth.

The wet heat, the strong suction, and the brush of his tongue combined to make Tamara cry out as a bolt of pure sensation shot through her.

Henry tilted her head up and back, and Tamara turned so she could brush her lips against his. He cupped her chin and took her mouth with his, hot and wet and carnal. With his tongue he stroked her deeply, an in-and-out penetration that gave her a hint of the actions his cock would soon take when he fucked her cunt.

Morgan let her nipple go with a wet plop, then gently blew air on her dampened flesh. Tamara shivered, and he chuckled.

Henry weaned his lips from hers and nuzzled her neck. His face rested beside hers as he looked over her shoulder. She never would have imagined it would turn her on, one man watching another play with her. Tamara had the feeling that before this night was done, she'd learn a lot of things about herself she'd never known.

"Did you know I can smell your cunt? It's been calling to me for hours." Morgan slid his hands under the loosened waistband of her jeans, then smoothed jeans and panties down her legs. He knelt before her and gently lifted one foot, and then the other, freeing her of her clothing.

He inhaled deeply, and Tamara moaned, the idea that he would inhale her somehow seeming more intimate an act than anything she'd ever known.

"Just like with a very fine wine. First you inhale the bouquet," he reached out and eased her legs just a little bit farther apart, "and then you sip."

Morgan said those last four words against the wet folds of her pussy. His lips settled on her, and he suited actions to words.

"Oh, God." The stroke of his tongue against her slit, up and down, back and forth, shot her arousal high and fast. Her heart thudded and her flesh pebbled. Her breathing hitched and her hips convulsed, pushing her pussy against his face.

Henry held her securely so that when her legs gave way he supported her. Then one hand left her middle to once more urge her lips to his. She gave him what he wanted with wild abandon.

Sleek and sultry, the wet and wonderful glide and slide of tongues, in her mouth, in her cunt, together, two men stroking her, drinking from her and pleasuring her, pushed Tamara's heat, her arousal to levels she'd never have believed possible. The sensations rushed at her hard and fast, stealing her breath.

Close, so close to coming, she turned her head away from Henry's kiss and into his shoulder. The sound that emerged from deep inside her seemed foreign to her own ears.

The men understood it instantly.

Henry reached down and pulled her nipple, pinching it lightly between his thumb and forefinger. Sharp, sudden, the pinch just edged her higher.

Then Morgan inserted two fingers into her pussy at the same time he sucked her clit into his mouth.

Tamara came so hard and so fast she screamed. Ecstasy flooded her, her body's contractions so strong, so overpowering she could only clench and reach and cry and shake as wave after wave of erotic bliss consumed her.

She gave no thought to anything but the pleasure, the pure, absolute ecstasy that filled her body, an electric blue avalanche of sensation that went on and on.

Seconds or hours later, Morgan gently tapered his ministrations then sat back on his haunches. He grinned up at her, his face wet from her juices, and as she watched him, he licked his lips.

"Give me some of that."

She could see her demand pleased him. He pushed to his feet then bent down, kissing her, lifting her so that he held her aloft and in his arms.

She tasted herself and him, and the combination of her body's dew and Morgan thrilled her. She wrapped her arms and legs around him. The hard ridge of his cock teased her. She ended their kiss and then ground her hips on him, rubbing her pussy against his denim-covered cock. She'd never had this happen—to have a stupendous orgasm and *still* crave more.

A strong male hand stroked her back. "Come here, Itty. Let me hold you while Morgan joins us."

Tamara looked over her shoulder and nearly gasped.

Tall, strong, completely aroused, Henry Kendall had shed his clothes and held his arms out to her.

She felt like a kid being passed from one adult to another. They weren't all that much taller than her, but they were a hell of a lot stronger.

"Somebody better fuck me soon." She grinned because her comment elicited laughter from both men.

"We're going to shower together. And then we're going to fuck you, Red." Morgan stripped out of his clothes in very short order.

"Or maybe," Henry said, "we'll do both at the same time."

Beautifully naked, erotically, totally male, Tamara looked from one Kendall to the other and licked her lips. They were buff, they were built, and they were fun to be with.

And for the next little while, at least, they were all hers.

Chapter 9

Tamara had never showered with a man before, and here she was about to indulge in that pleasure with two of them.

Steam curled around them, the heat magnifying the scent of sex they'd brought under the spray with them. Henry gently turned her so the flow of water missed her face.

Morgan joined them, setting something up on the soap tray. And then he turned on the other nozzles.

"Oh wow! *Four* showerheads?" Two were located high, at either end of the shower enclosure. The other two were at about waist height, under the higher ones. The sensation of water raining on her from so many nozzles felt *wonderful*.

"Mm. Don't worry. We have an extra large, high-efficiency water heater. And the nozzles don't stream as much water as you think."

Tamara laughed, because she'd just been going to ask if they had to wash quickly or be in danger of running out of hot water. The humorous and the mundane smoothed a moment that might have been awkward, otherwise.

It simply floored her how well these two flyboys seemed to know her already.

Henry stood behind her, his front flush against her back, his fully erect cock rubbing against the crack of her ass and the small of her back. It felt good to lean into him and rub back and forth against him.

"Mm." Henry wrapped an arm around her and returned the favor, stroking his cock back and forth against her ass.

"Oh, *yes*." She loved the feeling of that hot, hard shaft moving against her. These two brothers had kept her aroused since the night before, despite the explosive orgasms they'd given her. She *really* wanted them.

"I think our woman wants our cocks," Henry said.

Morgan had the soap in his hands and lathered them. Then he passed the bar to Henry.

"Soon, Red." Morgan put his hands on her breasts and began to wash her. "Very soon you'll have us all you want."

The sensation of Morgan's wet, soapy hands on her naked flesh gave her shivers and tingles and just plain made her go weak in the knees. Thank God Henry still had one arm around her waist. She'd have collapsed into a boneless heap on the shower floor, otherwise.

Morgan smoothed his hands across her breasts, then down, using his fingers to spread the soap over her slit and between her folds. Up and down the length of her pussy, he made thorough work of washing her.

"That feels so good." Her words came out on a moan.

"I'm glad," Morgan said. "Tilt your head back, honey."

She did, and he moved so the stream of water from the nozzle behind him caressed her flesh, rinsing away the suds.

"Come here." He coaxed her into his arms, and she understood it was so that his brother could take a turn bathing her.

Henry washed her hair, his fingers massaging with a touch that felt better than the best salon treatment. Tamara hadn't known until that moment that she could purr. She didn't even mind the smug-sounding masculine chuckles both men treated her to. Between them, they'd made her feel so good she figured they'd earned the right to be a little smug.

Henry smoothed his hand down her back, caressing across her bottom. Then he ran his fingers up and down the crack of her ass, stroking the tiny rosette of her anus, pushing on it slightly.

Tamara sucked in a breath while her bottom pushed back against the gentle touch, seeking more.

"Mm, you're very sensitive here, aren't you? Have you ever taken a cock in your ass, Tamara?" Henry asked.

"Never." Only one former lover had ever made the suggestion, and he'd turned out to be such a selfish son of a bitch, she'd told him flat-out, "No way."

"Will you take ours?" Morgan leaned over and kissed her. "We'll prepare you, first. We'll stretch you and play with you. Then..." He stroked his fingers over her slit and slid one deep inside her. "Then, if you find you like that, and if you let us, we'll both be able to fuck you at the same time."

"*Oh God.*" It took no effort to see that, to imagine that. The suggestion—dark, dangerous, and forbidden—slicked her sex and made her nipples bead. She would have sworn that she would never want to try anal sex. But just a whisper of a suggestion from these men and her body craved the invasion, the double penetration.

"You're going to drive me insane." She wondered at the fine trembling that shot through her. Her need for them had grown so huge, so fast, she shook with it. "Oh, please, *do* something. I need..." How could a body need like this? How could she, who'd always considered sex to be a so-so experience, often only tolerable after several good, stiff drinks, want to have sex with these men so very desperately?

Henry turned her to face him. "Hush, sweet baby. Don't beg. We want to give you anything you want and everything you need." He kissed her, and Tamara felt his trembling. Morgan stroked her, wrapped his arms around her from behind, and she knew then this desperation, this quaking hunger wasn't hers alone.

"Do you want to dry off and climb onto that big bed, or do you want me to take you here and now from behind?" Morgan's question whispered against her ear. The words shocked her and thrilled her at the same time.

"Here. Now. Oh God, hurry!"

"Then bend over for me, Red." The deep timbre of Morgan's voice teased the pit of her stomach, the rumble setting off even more sparks of excitement inside her. "Bend over so I can fuck you."

Henry moved to the side, took her hands, and placed them on the wall of the shower. She heard the tear of foil and imagined the slither of latex being rolled into place.

Bent from the waist, she looked over her shoulder and had one glimpse of Morgan's sheathed cock just before he took it in hand and placed it against her wet folds.

Oh, yes. The sensation of his hot cock brushing the lips of her pussy made her cunt release even more of her juices. He nudged her, seeking the right spot, and then he entered her, one slow, solid thrust that seated him deep within her body.

"Oh, Morgan, you feel so *good* inside me." His cock fit her as if he'd been made for her. She felt full, wonderfully, perfectly full.

"Damn you're hot and tight, Red." His words emerged as little more than a whisper, as if he wanted to focus everything on enjoying the sensations, with little energy left over for talking.

Morgan began to move inside her, his thrusts slow and steady, pulling almost all the way out of her, and then sliding into her again. Over and over he gave her those long, delicious strokes. The friction felt so good, she only wanted more and more and more. The desperation that had been eating at her calmed the moment his cock entered her. Her body patient now, arousal began a gentle and joy-filled climb.

"My God, how that turns me on, watching him fuck you." Henry's awe-filled tone added another dimension to the moment.

She looked up at him, and when his gaze met hers, she said, "I want to suck your cock."

"Tamara." He stepped just a bit closer, and she reached out with one hand and stroked his stiff shaft. When he closed his eyes on a groan, she opened her mouth and took him inside.

She loved the slide of his flesh in her mouth, the flavor tangy and good. She used her tongue to stroke at the same time she used her mouth to suck, tiny little pulses of suction that she could tell, by the way he moaned and then combed his fingers through her hair, felt good to him.

"Talk about a turn-on," Morgan said. "Damn, woman, you look good with cock in your mouth."

He began to move in her faster, the power of his plunges strong and deep. Tamara flexed her inner muscles, using her Kegel exercises to give Morgan's cock a rippling caress. At the same time, she sucked harder on Henry's.

"I'm close, baby," Henry said.

Tamara appreciated the warning, even though she ignored it. She caressed him faster, took him deeper, letting him know she wanted to drink him. She trailed her fingers down to stroke and tease his scrotum. Henry groaned and shivered.

Morgan's thrusts became sharper, and the slap of his balls against her slit excited her even more. Her own climax shimmered, so close, almost within reach.

Then Morgan reached around her. His fingers brushed where they joined, seeking, then finding her clit. He stroked it, teased it, and then pinched it tightly.

Tamara's climax burst inside her, the waves of rapture filling her with sparkling shivers of sensation. She moaned around Henry's cock, unwilling to release him, drawing pleasure from his presence there.

"Yes!" Henry's hands flexed as he held her head closer. His cock convulsed. The first spurt of his cream hit her throat and she drank, drawing his seed out of him. When she'd taken her second gulp, she felt Morgan stiffen and hold himself deep inside her. His cock throbbed in her pussy with his ejaculation. The heat of his semen filled the tiny pouch at the end of the condom, and that heat, against her cervix, made her orgasm peak anew.

Tamara would have collapsed if Morgan hadn't held her. Henry eased his cock out of her mouth, then bent over and kissed the top of her head. With her heart pounding she chased her breath as tiny aftershocks shot through her. "Holy crap."

"Well said, Itty." Henry reached out and turned off the water. "I vote we move this party to the bed."

"Definitely a good idea," Morgan said, "since we're no way near done yet."

In the past, Tamara had only wanted to sleep—alone—after having an orgasm. Of course, in the past she'd had to struggle just to come.

This time, and with these men, all she wanted was more.

* * * *

Morgan bit back his smile as he dried Tamara. No doubt about it, the woman wasn't used to being taken care of, not at all.

He and Henry would have to see what they could do about that. He supposed his feelings on the subject were a by-product of being raised in the family he had, and in the town he had.

The men of Lusty cherished their women. They took care of them, protected them, and yes, spoiled them. The behavior and attitude went all the way back to his ancestors, Adam Kendall and Warren Jessop, and Caleb and Joshua Benedict.

To Morgan's way of thinking, that was a fine tradition to claim.

"What's that look for?" Tamara's nose scrunched up, and her eyes narrowed as if by close scrutiny, she could read his mind.

He hoped there'd come a day when she could.

"I was thinking that you're not used to being pampered."

"No, I'm not."

She gave a little squeak when he picked her up, but she very quickly wrapped herself around him, her arms and legs an enticing clamp.

Her pretty little pussy perched low enough on his body to get his cock's attention. He forestalled further conversation by kissing her, then carrying her into the bedroom.

He set her down at the foot of the bed.

"Come here, Itty, and lay with me." Henry lay sprawled on the bed. He held his hand out to her, and Tamara immediately went to him, crawling up the mattress until she reached him then kept going until she straddled him.

Morgan grinned at the way she rubbed that hot pussy of hers against his brother's cock. He knew exactly what Henry was feeling at that moment.

"Good thing you already had a rubber on," he said.

"Mm." Henry grasped Tamara's waist, lifted her, then impaled her.

They both moaned in pleasure. Morgan stretched out on the bed beside them.

"Squeeze me, baby. Let me feel your inner muscles…mm, yes just like that."

"She has a wonderful cunt," Morgan said.

"God, yes. Wait until you feel her mouth."

"Gentlemen, I'm *right* here."

"You certainly are, my sweet, and incredibly easy to tease," Henry said.

"Now is *not* the time for teasing." Tamara's words emerged on a long sigh.

Morgan reached up and caressed Tamara's right breast as she rode his brother. Her movements, lithe and sensuous, spoke eloquently of her arousal.

Her eyes closed, her head thrown back as she surrendered to the physical, had any woman ever looked more alluring?

He continued to stroke her breast. Her skin felt soft, hot and so tempting that he wanted nothing more than to sink into her, melt into her completely.

Henry reached up and squeezed her other breast. "One time, I'd like to try and make you come just by playing with your breasts," he said.

"You two just might be able to do that," Tamara said. "Mm, I love both your cocks. They're just the right size for me. This feels so good. Never mind that I'm horny and going to come soon…above that, being fucked feels good."

"It's that way for us, too, when we can hold off our orgasm and just move inside you," Morgan said.

"Hanging just on the edge." Henry's voice sounded strained.

Morgan knew his brother was exactly there. He got up on his right knee, with his left foot flat on the bed, knee bent. He wanted more than just to watch. He wanted to feel Tamara's sexy mouth on his cock.

"Red."

Tamara opened her eyes and gave him a slow, sultry smile. She focused her gaze on his cock, and damned if that look didn't make him even harder. She leaned closer and fisted him, giving him two incredible strokes. And then, *yes*, she took his cock into her mouth.

He sank into her, hot and wet and wonderful. Morgan closed his eyes, the sensation of her suction sending shivers throughout his entire body. Slow and steady she drew him in. It was all he could do to hold himself from thrusting into her mouth with reckless abandon. He combed his fingers through the short cap of her hair, loving the silky slide of her tresses. He thought the guttural, soul-deep sounds emerging from his throat told her how much he loved what she was doing, but he wanted to give her the words.

"God, woman, that feels so incredibly good."

She smiled around his cock then groaned herself.

Morgan looked down, the scene so erotically moving. His brother, eyes wide, nearly glazed, fixed on the sight of their woman sucking cock. Morgan knew firsthand what a turn-on that was.

"Let's do this together." Henry reached up, stroked Tamara's breast, then trailed his hand down her body to just above where he entered her.

Henry stroked her clit, back and forth, and Tamara groaned. She sucked harder on Morgan's cock, and he gave in to the urge and pumped into her mouth, enticing ecstasy.

"Oh, God, yes." Henry's shout signaled his climax. He gripped Tamara's hips and held her close.

Tamara's sexy sounds thrilled him as she, too, reached her release.

Closing his eyes, Morgan let the rapture claim him as he came in a flood of the hottest pleasure he'd ever known.

Chapter 10

"No one's here, sir. Also, we've checked and the barn is empty, too."

Preston Rogers got out of his Buick Regal and peeled the sunglasses from his face. He took a moment to study Dennis' expression, and then he turned his gaze toward the house.

"House is locked up, but the barn wasn't. It's completely empty, sir. Kind of strange for a farm if you ask me."

"Yes, I agree. All right, let's move quickly. Can you unlock the house for me?"

"Yes, sir, no problem," Dennis assured him.

Fortunately, the house and barn were hidden not only from neighbors, but from the state road by means of a long driveway and a small hillock, and some trees that formed a natural protective barrier from prying eyes.

Of course, that protection also meant that they wouldn't be able to see anyone returning, either. He had no desire to be caught red-handed by Mr. Smith as he searched the man's home.

Preston leaned close to his driver, Lorne. "I want you to drive out to the road and then park along it down from the lane. Let us know if anyone approaches. Be ready to come get me when I call."

"Yes, sir."

Preston followed Dennis to the house. Jimmy, the man Preston considered his second and the most intelligent of his men, waited, his gun drawn, his gaze scanning the area.

Dennis had the house's front door open in under ten seconds. Preston nodded and clasped his shoulder. "I want you to have a look around that barn, and the fields beyond. See if you can find anything that might tell us something about the Piper."

Dennis nodded and headed off. Preston entered the house, Jimmy behind him. They had their guns drawn, just in case the place really wasn't deserted.

As he walked through the rooms, though, Preston thought the place *felt* empty.

"Mr. John Smith isn't much of a housekeeper, is he?" Preston shook his head. The place looked like it hadn't been cleaned in a decade or more. He felt his skin crawl the further into the building he ventured.

"And because there's all this crap all over the damn place, there's no way to know if the man went for beer, or simply left," Jimmy said.

The two-story farmhouse boasted only one room upstairs that had furniture. The other two rooms were filled with boxes and crates and God knew what else.

"Must be one of those pathological hoarders I've read about," Jimmy said.

"Well, there're some clothes in the closet, but not a lot. Huh, one of his dresser drawers is completely empty." Preston closed the drawer, careful to leave no prints. That was the biggest clue they had so far that the man might be gone for more than a few minutes.

Downstairs in what at one time had been a stylish dining room, on one end of the table, was the only item in the house not covered in filth and grime. The computer looked incongruous on the table, the sole nod to modern times the house contained.

"Huh. Damn near state-of-the-art. It's turned off and cool, so it's been off for a while," Jimmy said. Then he turned the computer on.

"Christ, I don't even know where else to look for anything. I'm half afraid of getting bitten by something or picking up some disease if I go through any of these piles of papers," Preston said.

"Let's hope he doesn't clean anything up in here, either," Jimmy said. "If his cookies and temporary Internet files are intact, we should be able to know something soon."

The kitchen door opened. Preston spun around, gun aimed, then lowered it when Dennis appeared in the doorway.

"I think I found something, boss. You'll want to come and take a look at this."

Preston stepped outside and breathed deeply. He had a feeling he was going to have the suit he was wearing cleaned after today's little adventure.

He followed Dennis as the man led him away from the house. Beyond the barn a pasture of grass spread out for what had to be acres. The Abilene area had seen some rain in the last week, more than what was normal for the month of November. The field felt soft to walk on and had obviously been even softer a few days before.

Preston looked down at the tracks, apparently made by a large, heavy truck. "No way of knowing when these tracks were made for sure, but I'm thinking after last Monday." Missed it by a couple of days. *If he'd gotten here a couple of days earlier, he'd have been successful. I was so fucking close to grabbing that plane.*

Several feet away were indentations in the grass made by two single tires, about four feet apart. He followed those across the field, away from the barn, until they simply stopped.

"Fuck." He had no doubt at all those tracks were made by the Piper when it lifted off. He headed back toward the barn. "Likely a gas truck," he said, pointing to the heavier tracks.

"Can't be that many companies that make those kinds of deliveries," Dennis said. "Maybe we can track them down. They would have a name, wouldn't they? Doubtful the farmer here paid for the gas. That would be on whoever picked up the plane."

"I think you'd be surprised how many companies there are, but yeah, good thinking." He could chase that down, of course, and would. He headed back into the house.

"Anything yet, Jimmy?"

"It appears Mr. Smith has taken a vacation. He grabbed a last-minute deal from an Internet travel agent. The man has flown off to Miami. Plane left just this morning, in fact. There he'll board a cruise ship."

"Well, since he won't be back, let's take this pile of shit with us. You can work your magic on it and see if you can find out where the plane went."

"He has a Money Buddy account because he has the site bookmarked. Don't worry, sir, if there's a money trail to be found, I'll find it."

Preston pulled out his cell phone to call Lorne. "Find it fast, Jimmy. If we don't get our hands on that Piper soon, Ramos will see to it we're all nothing more than rotting carcasses left in the desert as carrion."

* * * *

Tamara awoke to the delicious sensation of having her pussy licked.

The slow slide of a wet tongue along the edges of her labia, the slight flirty dip into the entrance beyond, and the teasingly close flick next to her clit drew her from sleeping to wakefulness in mere seconds.

She groaned even before she'd become fully alert, the undulation of her hips an automatic response to the delightful stimulation she was receiving.

"Good morning." Morgan paused long enough to look up and flash her a cheeky grin.

She met his gaze and returned his smile. "It certainly is. My two favorite fantasies…sex, overlaid with the scent of coffee and bacon."

"I'm so glad you said 'sex' first, sweetheart. Proves you have your priorities in the right place. Henry's making breakfast, and I'm making you."

Tamara had a smart answer on the tip of her tongue. Morgan surged up her body and thrust his cock into her pussy and his tongue into her mouth.

Smart-ass answers gave way to a sudden spike in arousal. Words evaporated in the rising heat of mutual lust. Tamara gave herself to the all-out physical thrill. Moving in sync with the man on her and in her, she stretched and pressed and rubbed, moving her hips in counterpoint to his.

Their tongues dueled, a dance of knowing, a tango of teasing. She could taste them both, and the flavor was dark, a forbidden ambrosia that fueled her fire and primed her passion.

Morgan slid one hand under her bottom, urging her closer, and she wrapped her legs around him, rubbing her pussy close and fast against his groin.

Her clit made contact with the hair cradling the base of his cock, and she shivered with the delicious sensation. Her climax beckoned. Tamara's heart raced toward it, and her blood burned for it.

"Come with me, Tamara. Let's fly together."

He had only to say the words and she felt it begin, the dizzying climb, higher and then higher still. No, this wasn't about flying, she understood in a heartbeat, but falling, a vast, exciting, meteoric free fall from the very acme of arousal down the chute of ecstasy into a hot, bubbling cauldron of bliss.

Yes, a fall, not flying, and God help me, I've fallen hard.

The orgasm shot through her, shredding her emotional defenses even as it sent electrifying pleasure out to every part of her body. The shivers of her climax shattered her and made her whole again at the same time. Above her, Morgan stiffened, letting loose her lips and groaning as his cock convulsed inside her. His orgasm caressed hers from the inside, making it longer, stronger, and more.

Making it much more than just an orgasm.

The rapture began to fade, and in its wake lassitude crept over her, lulling her with a sense of contentment, luring her into the need to cling. How easy it would be to give in, to take and to revel and hold on without thinking.

Morgan rolled to his side and brought her with him, his arms cradling her.

"What's wrong, Red?"

How could she answer him without giving away even more of her soul? This man and his brother had drilled through all the protective layers she'd spent a lifetime building around her heart. Now the remnants of those layers were falling away, leaving her open and so very vulnerable.

"What makes you think anything's wrong?" She thanked her ingrained habit of denial for giving her a moment or two to think.

"I feel your sadness." He moved then, easing her onto her back. His gaze, when it met hers, had filled with tenderness. "You have to know Henry and I would never hurt you. You're safe with us."

"Maybe you wouldn't mean to hurt me." *Damn.* Couldn't she keep anything in when it came to these damn Kendalls?

"It's all right, sweetheart. We'll just take things one day at a time." He used a hand to stroke her hair off her face and to caress her cheek. "We're not asking you to give us anything you're not ready to give us, or anything you don't want to."

Shows how much he knows. Because he seemed to want one, she gave him a small smile. Then, since his gaze saw far too much, she stretched up and laid her lips on his, hoping to distract him.

He kissed her back sweetly, then weaned his lips from hers and continued to stare at her.

Tamara knew she'd already given these two flyboys something she'd never intended to let them anywhere near. She'd given them her heart.

"Breakfast is likely ready, or just about," Morgan said. "What do you say we eat first and then shower?"

"No, you go ahead. I'll just grab a quick shower on my own. I'll be down in a few minutes."

Morgan looked at her for a long moment, and inside herself, Tamara fought the urge to squirm. Then he leaned over her and gave her another quick kiss.

"You can run, Red, but you can't hide. You're bound to try, though. I feel it only fair to warn you that we aren't going to give up on you." He held her gaze and seemed to be looking for something within the depths of her eyes. "Baby, you don't need to hide from us."

"You don't understand. You don't know where I'm coming from. It's easy for you to say that, to feel that. Everything is so simple for you. Look at the family you grew up in!" She had to get away from him before he broke her down completely. She felt too close to something she'd never considered having, too close to being completely naked in a way that felt far more threatening than simply being without her clothes.

"You mean because I have three fathers?" A slight chill had entered his voice, and it would likely be smart to let him think that. It would be the perfect way to get back the ground she'd lost. Let him and Henry both think she was turned off by his family, by their lifestyle.

Oh yes, it would be easy, but she simply couldn't do that. *Why do I have to be so damned honest?*

"No. Because your parents are still together and still in love."

For a long moment Morgan simply looked at her. "You're right that we don't know you, Henry and I, and we don't know where you're coming from. But Red? We're going to, probably sooner than you'll be comfortable with."

She already was uncomfortable with the speed with which these two men had taken her from the purely physical to so very much more. "One day at a time, you said. And this one is going to start with my having a shower, *alone*." She would cling to that. She'd buy herself a tiny bit of space, and she'd shore up her defenses as best she could.

If she wanted to keep her dignity intact and her vulnerability protected, she really had no choice in the matter.

"Okay." Morgan kissed her lightly then bounded out of bed. He made a very quick trip to the bathroom—likely to dispose of the condom—and then waltzed back into the bedroom, completely naked and easy with it.

Tamara knew it was very silly to hold the sheet up over her body. He'd seen, touched, and kissed every inch of her. None of that mattered. She clutched the exquisite cotton close. *Desperate times really did call for desperate measures.*

She watched him stroll naked over to one of the dressers. He grabbed a pair of boxers and a T-shirt out of a drawer then scooped his jeans off the floor. With clothing in hand he headed toward the stairs. She almost sighed with relief when he reached the doorframe. Then he turned around and gave her a very cheeky grin.

"But I should point out that your day already has begun and, baby, you definitely weren't alone when it happened." He winked then headed toward the stairs.

Tamara flopped back down on the pillow and wondered which urge warring within her would win—the one to scream, or the one to laugh.

Chapter 11

"Hey, don't apologize, Jordan. There's nothing you can do about it. We'll just work harder tomorrow."

Morgan closed his cell phone then turned when he heard the sound of Tamara's step on the stairs. He waited until she appeared in the door of the kitchen before saying, "That was Jordan. The material he ordered isn't going to make it in until late afternoon."

"Well, hell," Henry said as he reached into the oven and began to pull out plates of food. "I wonder what we'll do to fill our day *now*?"

Since he slid a grin to their woman when he said that, Tamara smiled. "Maybe you can refine your business plan and draw up a prospectus."

"Now that sounds totally boring." Henry set two of the plates on the breakfast table. Tamara seemed to notice the food for the first time.

"You didn't have to wait for me."

"Don't be silly, Red. Of course we did. Come and eat."

The first few moments were filled with distributing the food and pouring coffee.

"Actually," Henry said, "we probably should spend some time on our business plan. But to be honest with you, Morgan and I are both hands-on. We figured once we got going, we'd have to hire someone to do the paperwork and fly the desk, so to speak."

Tamara grinned. "I hear you. Actually, that's where I'm lucky. My business partner loves the paperwork, and flying a desk comes very naturally to him."

"You went to live with your great-uncle when you were still a kid?" Morgan wanted to draw Tamara out. She'd hit the nail on the head earlier when she'd said they didn't know her. At least as far as the details of her life were concerned.

He could have argued that he and Henry did know her, deep inside and in a way that was damn near spiritual. However, he sensed she wasn't ready to hear anything quite that deep yet.

"Yes. My parents were still playing 'pass the kid,' I had just turned sixteen, and I'd had enough. I'd met Uncle Goodwin—my mother's uncle—a couple of years before when he'd come to visit."

"So you hadn't known him long?" Henry asked.

"No, but that was totally not his fault. Mom kept moving us, wherever she thought the fishing might be better. She never stayed with anything, a job or a man, for long. Usually she'd move us after a relationship ended. Uncle Goodwin had been looking for us for quite a while."

"So you banked on him taking you in?" Morgan asked.

"Yeah. Dad's most recent girlfriend considered me competition—I mean, she was only about four years older than me at the time—so Dad said I had to go back and live with Mom."

"And instead you knocked on your uncle's door." Henry grinned at her.

Tamara's smile turned soft. "He opened the door, saw my suitcase, and said, 'It's about damn time.'" She grinned. "So right then and there I moved in. About a month later we moved from the double-wide trailer he was in to a small hobby farm that had been for sale. It had a solid, brick house with a yard, room for a garden, and a small barn he said was good for tinkering in."

"He moved you from what many might consider a temporary home, to a permanent one," Morgan said.

Tamara blinked. "Huh. I never looked at it that way before. But I think you're right. That's exactly what he did."

"We'd like to meet him some time," Henry said. "He sounds like a man worth knowing."

"He is. He's getting older." Tamara blinked, and Morgan wondered if she realized how much of herself she revealed in her tone and expressions. "One of his best friends passed away last year, and another one moved to Florida to be closer to his family. He'd been pretty down until he hit on this idea of starting a crop-dusting service."

"He must have gotten the idea from his friend who sold him the Piper," Henry said.

Tamara shrugged. "To be honest with you, I'm not sure where the idea came from. But you'd have to know my uncle to understand that. No one can come up with more ideas on how to make a buck than Goodwin Hornsby. But we've always managed to make do."

"Your uncle is Goodwin Hornsby?" Morgan looked over at Henry, who immediately raised one eyebrow.

Tamara had her gaze on her food as she forked a bit of potato. "Like I said, he's my mom's uncle. Jones is my father's side of the family."

He looked at her to see if she was being a smart-ass, if she'd been speaking facetiously. When she tilted her head and said, "What?" Morgan realized that she didn't know one aspect of her great-uncle at all.

If the man hadn't bothered to disclose his business reputation to his niece, Morgan wasn't going to be the one to do so. At least not yet, though he would hold that in reserve. After all, his loyalty lay with his woman, not her kin.

"There was a Colonel Hornsby, RAF, in Afghanistan," Henry said, proving he was on the same page as Morgan. "Any relation, do you think?" Henry's expression looked completely guileless. Morgan could only admire his brother's quick mind.

"Maybe way back. I think my uncle's antecedents came from England."

"Ah, so maybe the Colonel was a far and removed distant cousin," Henry said.

"Could be." A surprised look crossed her face when she looked down at her plate and saw that it was empty.

"So now that breakfast is over, what do you want to do?"

Morgan had to smile at the tone Henry used. He sounded innocent as hell, which, of course, he wasn't.

"I guess since you cooked, I should do the dishes," Tamara said.

"No, I think Morgan can do the cleanup while you and I cook…upstairs."

"But I just had a shower!" Tamara's pout wasn't convincing at all.

"Ah, but did you soak in the Jacuzzi yet?"

"I knew there was something I forgot to do."

Henry grinned and extended his hand to her as he got to his feet. "Don't worry, Itty Bitty. I'll take care of you."

"I just bet you will."

She looked over at Morgan, her head tilted to the side. He understood she was asking how he felt about her going off to have some private time with Henry. Eventually she'd become more comfortable with their arrangement. Eventually she'd come to understand that he and his brother would never be jealous of each other. But that, of course, would take time.

"Go have fun," he said. "I'll be up later."

He counted it a good sign that she flashed a quick look below his belt and giggled.

* * * *

Tamara wouldn't have thought she could be horny again so soon. She mentally shook her head. All Henry had to do was suggest getting naked and wet, and she got wet. *Could I be any easier?*

He kept a hold of her hand as he led her through the bedroom to the bathroom. He walked straight over to the tub where he turned on the Jacuzzi jets. Turning to face her, he brought her hand up to his mouth and kissed it. His slow, sweet smile turned her resolve to mush and made her smile right back at him.

"How long until that hot tub gets hot?" Tamara had never actually indulged in a Jacuzzi, but considering the activities of the night before she thought the spa might prove to be the perfect therapy for muscles that ached slightly from unaccustomed activity.

"It takes a couple of hours when you first fill it, but then it stays hot. At least ours does. We Kendalls take our water sports very seriously. One never knows when one might want to…play."

He drew her forward until she stood flush against him. When he wrapped his arms around her waist, she looped hers around his neck.

"Yesterday afternoon, I filled it and even had champagne chilling in a bucket close at hand."

"We never made it out of bed to indulge last night."

"No, we didn't, but I can't really complain. We *did* drink the wine, if you'll recall."

Tamara felt her insides melting just thinking about the way the men had lapped bubbly from her breasts and stomach.

"I most definitely do recall. That was another new experience for me." She stopped speaking so she could stretch up and place a tiny kiss on his lips. "I've been really racking them up in the last twenty-four hours." Tamara loved the way Henry moved his hands slowly up and down her back. Something about the way both he and Morgan touched her felt so good.

"You seem to be coping well with that realization." He leaned down and returned the favor, placing a chaste kiss on her lips.

"It's not just the things we've done together that are new. It's the way I feel doing them. I used to believe that sex was no big deal, and that all the fireworks and heat I'd heard about nothing more than hype. You're the first men who've really turned me on. It's like—" Tamara stopped mid sentence. *Why do I keep running off at the mouth with these Kendalls?* Crap, if she wasn't careful, she'd have no secrets left at all.

"It's like what, sweetheart?"

If he'd teased, if he'd put on that cheeky grin he often used when he asked her a question, she might have been able to come up with a coy one-liner of her own in response—something trite to steer them out of emotional territory. But how did she fight the effect of that patient, tender look? How could she be glib as she so often was when he looked at her as if she was the center of the universe and her next words its most treasured truth?

"It's as if my emotions were sleeping until the two of you came along and woke them up."

"Shh." Henry brought one arm from around her waist. She didn't even realize she was crying until he wiped a tear from her cheek.

"You feel confused, off balance, as if your world has been turned upside down in the course of a couple of days. I can tell you without a word of a lie, Tamara, that it's the same for us."

"You don't act off balance, or confused." She regretted that slight note of accusation in her tone. "You two flyboys have seemed completely self-possessed from the moment I fell out of the sky and landed practically in your laps."

"Waiting for you to come home yesterday afternoon, my stomach clenched, I was so nervous. I kept checking to make sure I'd covered all the bases because you matter, Itty. And oh, look at that flash of panic in your eyes! You *do* matter, Tamara Jones, and you have since, as you put it, you fell out of the sky and into our laps. But don't worry, you don't have to do anything more with that fact right now except acknowledge it."

Before Tamara could launch a rebuttal or think of even one word to say, Henry tightened his arms around her, drew her in closer, and kissed her.

So good. His taste aroused her, the aroma of his masculinity surrounded and seduced her, and Tamara knew the sensation of flying without a plane.

His hands stroked up and down her body in sync with the stroking of his tongue against hers. Nestling closer, she felt the firm ridge of his penis as it pressed against her belly. That sensation alone made her pussy release moisture.

He kissed her as if there would only be this, as if the mating of mouths and the tangle of tongues was enough for him. Slow and sensuous, soft and sultry, his lips coaxed and wooed hers. Tamara felt completely charmed.

"I want to undress you and bring you into the froth with me." Henry's words caressed her moist lips. "I want to touch you and taste you and tease you." He eased back and cupped her face with his hands. "Will you let me have my way with you?"

"Since your way appears to be my way, too." Tamara could no more refuse him than she could stop from taking her next breath.

"Mm, is it? I want to play with your ass. I want to get you ready to take us, there."

She knew generally speaking what he meant, of course. Just the idea of having both these men inside her body at the same time caused a delightful shiver to course down her spine. She wasn't too clear on the specifics.

"Get me ready, how?"

Henry turned her so that her back cozied against his front. The press of his erection against her back made her hotter.

He put his lips close to the shell of her ear. "I'll run my fingers up and down the crack of your ass and see how you like that. If you do, then I'll dip into the lube I have here on the shelf and caress you with it, up and down, with increasing pressure, until I ease my fingers into your anus. Then, after I've stretched your pretty little rosebud just a little, I'll slide the first butt plug into you."

Henry's words stoked her fires, the erotic whisper a promise of dark, forbidden pleasures as yet untried. As his words teased her, his hands began to free her from her clothing.

"Darling, your nipples are very hard little buds. Tell me." He kissed her ear and tongued it, then licked the column of her neck. "Do you want me to play with your ass?" He licked the shell of her ear, and Tamara could have sworn her nipples just pinched tighter. "Do you want me to fuck your ass?"

The whimper that emerged from her throat sounded desperate, but she didn't care. She was desperate and getting more so by the moment. Henry finished undressing her, letting her clothes simply drop to the floor. Then he surrounded her with his arms and his heat.

How uniquely sexy it felt to be naked in the arms of a man who was fully clothed. A man whose hands knew exactly where and how to touch her in order to drive her wild.

"I like you, Tamara Jones, but I particularly like you naked, in my arms."

He turned her around and kissed her, a hot, wet, and very carnal kiss, a prelude to the other carnal delights in store for them both. His tongue devoured hers, sweeping in and claiming her mouth as a pirate would claim any willing wench. Tamara was more than willing. She was hot, eager, and horny.

Then Henry broke their kiss and lifted her into the churning water.

Chapter 12

Tamara appreciated the differences between her lovers. Morgan's sexuality was raw and elemental, while Henry's tended to be smoother and more urbane.

Except right now.

Henry stepped back from setting her in the tub and practically tore off his clothes. His rushed, eager movements made her smile and stroked her feminine ego. Maybe he'd told the truth when he said he and Morgan were as affected by this thing happening between them as she was.

Henry got into the spa and reached for her. Sometimes it suited her to let these men lead, and that did surprise her, because she never thought she'd want an alpha male bossing her around. Just lately she had two of them and liked that fact just fine.

Only right at the moment she was feeling a little aggressive herself.

She wound her arms around his neck and pressed her body close to his. She sighed when his arms enfolded her. "You feel so good against me. And when your arms come around me, it makes me quiver inside." She felt the same way when Morgan's arms surrounded her. Everything and anything these men did to and with her thrilled her in ways she'd never have guessed was possible.

Delightful friction kept her nipples hard as she rubbed her breasts back and forth across Henry's chest.

"Mmm, you've got me hard already."

"Good. I like it when you're hard. I want you to fuck me." She kissed him, her mouth ravenous to taste all of him, to share the heat and the lust racing through her.

In a heartbeat he took over, pulling her down onto his lap as he sat on the bench, opening her legs, and setting her astride him. His hot, engorged cock nestled between the folds of her pussy. Her clit poked up to join in the celebration, and the heat of his erection, just there on that sensitive bud, sent her arousal soaring.

He made his cock pulse so that it seemed to reach out and caress her. She grinned into his mouth and returned the greeting.

Then Henry reached around and stroked up and down over her anus, his fingers pressing slightly against the opening, and it was all she could do not to come right then and there.

Tamara broke their kiss to gasp, to rub against him, and to moan. Henry's deep, smug chuckle should have irked her, but the thrill of that touch, of the depth of her arousal and the need to experience it again, superseded everything.

"Itty, I am so glad you liked that." Henry nibbled on her neck, his tongue licking away the tiny sting of his nips.

"Do it again. Oh, God, do it again." She didn't care if she had to beg on hands and knees. Some things were worth any price, and that mini explosion of rapture was one.

"Don't worry. I guarantee you'll be totally satisfied before much longer." He gave her a quick little peck on her lips. "Hand her a condom, will you, Morgan?"

Tamara hadn't even noticed the other man come into the room. When he reached onto the shelf at the back of the spa and then handed her the packet, she took it and gave him a big smile.

Henry slid her off his lap so he could stand.

Tamara tore open the foil packet and withdrew the rolled-up sheath. Henry's cock felt hot and firm, and she had no trouble sliding the protection into place. Of course, she wanted to be very thorough, so she made her movements long and slow, with a few extra strokes just to make sure the prophylactic stayed where it needed to be.

"Vixen. Keep that up and I'm going to come in your hand before I even get inside you. Now come here. I want to feel your hot pussy around my cock."

Tamara reached for Henry at the same moment he put his hands on her waist and lifted her. She really didn't think she was *that* small of a woman, yet these flyboys kept picking her up as if she weighed nothing.

A part of her reveled in the display of their casual strength. She had no worries that either of the Kendall brothers would ever use that strength against her. She knew her body was safe with them even if she suspected her heart might not be.

Henry brought her down onto his cock, and she hummed in pure contentment as the hard male shaft slid silkily inside her.

"That feels so *good*." She began to ride him, a gentle up-and-down motion that would pleasure them both. She liked that both men had cocks that filled her nicely without stretching her overmuch. If they'd been designed especially for her, they couldn't have fit her any better.

"It does feel good. You feel good, all hot and wet and tight around me. Squeeze me, sweetheart." Henry kept his hands on her waist, helping her move. The look of enjoyment on his face gave her a kind of satisfaction that was nearly as good, in its way, as a climax.

Tamara flexed her pelvic floor muscles, giving Henry's cock an inner caress that she knew rippled the entire length of his shaft.

"Mm, *damn*, you're good."

The sound of a small splash made Tamara look over her shoulder. Morgan had stripped and gotten into the tub with them.

"She fits us as if she was made for us," Morgan said.

"Yes, she does." Henry's gaze locked with hers, his eyes twinkling.

"I'm in too good a place right now to be irked that you're talking as if I'm not even here," Tamara said.

"Sweetheart, if you weren't even here, this entire scene would be bizarre," Henry said.

Tamara laughed, loving the way Henry's not-so-latent smart-ass always surged to the fore.

"Let's see if we can make that place you're in even better," Morgan said.

The heat from his body warmed her back as he moved in close behind her. The sensation of being surrounded by these two virile males gave her a unique kind of buzz.

She moved up and down on Henry's cock while Morgan kissed her shoulder and back and reached around to stroke her left breast.

"Up a little, baby," Henry said.

He used his strength to hold her up so his cock barely penetrated her.

"Something cool," Morgan said.

Tamara gasped as Morgan trailed his fingers along the crack of her ass, his touch cool and silky as he spread the lube back and forth over her anus.

"Oh, yes." His touch there aroused her as much as his brother's had. She shivered because the erotic play gave her gooseflesh.

"A bit more cool. I'm going to penetrate you with my finger, Red. I don't want to hurt you too much. You can stop me with just one word. Okay?"

Tamara nodded, the movement jerky, because the caress along her anus was too exciting to allow for speech.

Morgan's fingers left her for just a moment, and then returned, the extra amount of lube he'd scooped making her shiver even more.

Henry leaned forward and took one nipple into his mouth and suckled hard. Tamara moved one hand from his shoulder to his head, holding him against her tender flesh so he'd know how much she loved his mouth on her.

Then he eased her down onto his cock again, and Morgan began to press against the opening of her anus.

Morgan moved to the side and nuzzled her cheek at the same time as he pressed his finger into her.

Tamara felt the slight burning but couldn't say that it hurt, exactly. The shivery excitement his earlier touch had given her returned but seemed to reach deeper inside her. The twinge of discomfort wrapped in arousal shot from her ass to her clit. She realized she'd stopped moving on Henry and that his cock was seated deep within her.

"Tamara."

She looked at Morgan in response to the sound of her name. His mouth was there, seeking. He settled his lips on hers and kissed her, his tongue insistent on stroking hers, tasting every bit of her. She felt Henry's mouth suckle her again, drawing hard. Someone stroked her clit, coaxing her orgasm to rush up and out of her.

The first wave broke over her, and Morgan pushed his finger all the way inside her.

"Oh, God!" It felt like two orgasms in one. Tamara began to shake with the force of it, the ecstasy so deep and rich, she didn't know if she could contain it all.

Henry's arms surrounded her as Morgan's finger kept moving inside of her.

"Just a bit more," he said.

More? She didn't know if she could take any more, but then she felt Morgan pull his finger out of her and she whimpered, wanting it back.

"Mmm, you do like this. Good." He kissed her ear and then stroked over her anus again. She could feel two fingers there and made a deep, humming sound when he began to push both of them into her.

"Your pussy just got tighter, Itty." Henry kissed the words against her neck. "Squeeze me again, baby. Ride me."

Tamara fastened her mouth on his as she did as he asked. Her tongue danced with his, an erotic, wet glide that stroked her passion as well as her lover's mouth, his taste fueling her fire. The sensation of Henry's cock moving in and out of her at the same time Morgan's fingers fucked her ass were incredibly arousing. *How can I need to come again so soon?* The last orgasm still tingled along her nerve endings, yet incredibly she felt another one building within her.

She pulled her mouth from Henry's, and the climb turned desperate. Her forehead resting on his, her motions turned sharp and fast, as she chased an orgasm that seemed determined to stay just out of her reach.

"Easy, baby." Morgan's whisper in her ear didn't make any sense. Then he took his fingers from her, and she wanted to scream with the frustration, with the sudden drop of Eros. "No no no no no! Please, go back I need...*oh, God, yes*!"

He hadn't left her, he'd returned with something large, something other, and slid it into her hungry hole. Once more someone found her clit and stroked it. This time, her orgasm exploded, a volcanic eruption that held her hard and fast as tremor after tremor racked through her.

"Jesus!" Henry's curse, the clamp of his arms and the pulsing of his cock inside her told her he came, too. The heat from his ejaculation softly battered her cervix.

Tamara knew one crazy moment of regret that a condom prevented conception.

"My God, watching you come turns me on," Morgan said. He kissed the side of her head and ran his hand up and down her back. He stepped away, and she immediately missed his heat.

Inside her, the butt plug remained a solid presence, not unpleasant but definitely unfamiliar. She flexed her inner muscles.

"Mercy," Henry said.

Tamara fought for breath and fought the urge to laugh. Then Morgan came back and wrapped his arms around her from behind.

"Come snuggle with me, Red."

"'Kay." She'd get up as soon as she felt there was some strength in her body to move. Lucky for her, Morgan simply lifted her into his arms. Then he sat on the bench and cradled her on his lap.

Slowly, her senses returned. She heard again the gurgling of the jets as they sent bubbles throughout the tub. She heard Henry get out of the spa and move about the bathroom.

"I'll boost the temperature a few degrees," he said.

"I thought it felt cooler than usual."

"You need a lift."

Tamara knew her words, spoken around a yawn, didn't make any sense.

"No, we're not going anywhere," Henry said as he climbed back into the tub.

"No. To take you out of the tub and dump you into bed. One of those electric ones where all you have to do is push buttons."

Morgan laughed. "Your first spa experience?"

"Mm." She nestled into him even more and totally relaxed. The orgasms and the heat of the water combined to make her feel boneless.

Morgan stroked down her back and across her bottom. "Does that feel okay inside you?"

"Mm. Different. But it doesn't hurt."

"Good. We won't leave it in for very long, this first time."

"I've never had an orgasm quite like that. It felt as if I was coming in two different places at the same time."

"Just think how good it's going to feel when you have both our cocks in you at the same time," he said.

"You're going to turn me into a quivering, shivering sex-addict." Both men chuckled, and that was fine. But from where she was sitting—naked on one lover's lap after being pleasured by both him and her other lover—the possibility didn't seem that farfetched.

"You didn't get much sleep last night, sweetheart. You need a nap." Henry kissed her shoulder.

The men shifted her slightly so that she lounged across both of their laps.

"Nap? It's not even noon yet." And the idea that she probably wasn't all that far from sliding into sleep mid-morning somehow tickled her.

"Tell you what. Why don't we get out, dry off, and snuggle in our bed? You don't have to take a nap if you don't want to." Morgan's husky voice settled low in her belly, and she wondered, as arousal began to stir gently, just how many times she could be brought to orgasm in a single day.

"And if we do doze off, so what?" Henry said.

"Unless you have something more pressing to do?" Morgan asked.

Tamara wiggled her hips, making contact with two cocks that didn't feel all that flaccid to her.

It didn't surprise her that Morgan was hard. He'd not joined in their little party of a few minutes before. That Henry could be stirring so soon made her wonder if she shouldn't start taking a multivitamin.

"Come to think of it, I do believe a couple of things are quite pressing at the moment."

"Maybe while we're all snuggled in our bed, those pressing matters will simply go away," Henry said.

Tamara heard just enough humor in his voice to make her smile.

"God, I hope not." Tamara resolved then and there to do her best to ensure that they didn't disappear without some serious attention, first.

Chapter 13

Jordan Kendall pulled on his carpenters' tool belt and grabbed a handful of nails. He'd chewed out his supplier for a good half hour, doing everything he could to try and expedite that shipment of sheet steel. Every once in a while a supplier would have a glitch, and while that was normal in construction, Jordan had been beyond pissed this time.

If he were to be honest with himself, he'd been a lot more pissed than the situation actually called for.

His mind settled on the obvious reason for his uncharacteristic short temper. This was a family build, and he wanted everything to go like clockwork.

Liar.

Yes, he was lying. But he was only lying to himself and whose business was it if he was? No one's, that's whose.

So he decided he needed to go pound some nails for a while. Pounding on nails—in lieu of pounding on his brothers, which he couldn't do now that he was supposed to be an adult—was the one thing guaranteed to work off some of his pissy mood.

The sound of a car approaching caught his attention. He swallowed hard and watched as the Crown Vic pulled up to the back of the helicopter hangar, next to his own Ford F-150.

Peter Alvarez stepped out of the car. The man took off the sunglasses he'd worn while driving, and hooked them into the *V* of his button-front shirt. Jordan couldn't look away from him and felt his heart give a jolt when Peter spotted him.

There's just something about the guy. Can't put my finger on what it is. My cop radar is vibrating.

Adam's words played back in his mind while Peter walked toward him. He could see that Peter's gaze fixed on the tool belt around Jordan's waist.

At least, that's where Jordan chose to think Peter's gaze rested.

"You said there'd be no work today."

"That's right." Jordan sighed. He heard the edge in his own voice and could have cursed his lack of control. More, Jordan understood why it was there, and by the look in Peter's eyes, he understood the reason, too.

"So no one else will likely come by? It'll likely be just you and me here for a while?"

"Yeah." It took all of Jordan's considerable will to not let his gaze skitter away from Peter's.

"Then we should talk, don't you think?"

"Yeah." *Christ, Kendall, could you be any more eloquent?* Jordan sighed. This wasn't like him at all. It had always been his nature to face whatever the hell life threw at him, square on. "Yes," he said again. "We should talk. I'll give you the nickel tour of the place. The Lear hangar has a lounge, and a vending machine."

"The *Lear* hangar?"

Jordan laughed. "The families have a habit of naming things. That one," he pointed to the far right, "is the Lear hangar. This one, the helicopter hangar, though actually it's only one building, divided in half by a wall."

"And the one we're building?"

"Future home of Kendall Aviation, as well as Benedict-Murphy Investigations." Jordan took off his tool belt and set it in the back of his truck. He began walking toward the back door of the helicopter hangar.

"Kendall Aviation. That would be your brothers, the ones who were here yesterday?" Peter followed him.

"That's right. Morgan and Henry both just retired from the Air Force. All things considered, it's only natural they'd go into business together."

"Ah."

Jordan unlocked and then opened the door to the building and held it for Peter to enter. "'Ah'?"

Peter grinned, and Jordan had to fight the effect that smile had on him. "The woman who was with them yesterday. She's *their* woman."

Jordan tilted his head slightly, trying to read Peter's meaning.

"Don't forget, I grew up hearing stories of the families, and this town," he said. "And now I understand the vibes I got from both men. They were protecting their woman."

Not censure, then. "It came as some surprise to my brothers when Tamara dropped out of the sky, but it didn't take them long to figure out that she *was* their woman. We'll have to see how long it takes them to convince her of that fact. And those wouldn't have been the only vibes you got from them. I'm younger, and they've always been a little protective."

"Understandable. Wait a minute. You said Tamara dropped out of the sky?"

"She did." Jordan fought his grin. He'd explain later. In the meantime, he could see no reason not to have a little fun.

Peter whistled when he got his first look at the helicopter. The EC120 B Colibri's paint was still shiny new. They hadn't had it all that long. Jordan hadn't been up in it yet, but Henry said she flew like a dream.

"This belongs to your family?" Peter asked.

"The families," Jordan corrected. "Or rather, technically, the airstrip and everything else on it belongs to the Lusty, Texas, Town Trust."

"The legal entity that Warren Jessop set up all those years ago to give them the space and the privacy they needed to live as they chose," Peter said. "I did a little research on top of hearing the stories from my *abuela*. My roots are here, and I've always been curious."

In Jordan's experience, those who were connected to Lusty but never visited could be just as loyal as those born here. He felt himself begin to relax, just a little. "Turns out my ancestor was a hell of a lawyer. That trust still stands today."

Jordan led Peter through the hangar and out the other side. Barely any space separated the two entrances. He unlocked the other door.

"Wow. You don't see many of these up close," Peter said. He took a moment to admire the Learjet 40XR. "How many people can she carry?"

"Two crew and seven passengers. The other one is bigger. It's in New York at the moment, being used by some of the family there."

"And what's this, the poor relation?" Peter pointed at the Piper sitting on the other side of the Lear.

Jordan laughed. "No. That's Tamara's Piper. Or I should say, her uncle's. She was ferrying it from Abilene to San Marcos when the engine decided to quit. We're just giving it shelter until she can get it fixed."

"The engine quit? My God, she had to land it dead-stick?"

Jordan nodded. "Sure as hell did. Morgan said she brought that baby in and set her down better than some air force pilots could have done."

"Must have scared the crap right out of her."

"You've got to figure." Jordan led the way over to the lounge, a comfortable-looking room with glass walls, a sofa, some easy chairs, and a couple of vending machines. He walked straight over to one of the machines. "Coffee?"

"Yes, please."

Jordan wondered if he heard suppressed laughter in the other man's voice, or if it was just his imagination.

"How do you take it?" Jordan closed his eyes at the unintentional double entendre. He supposed that no matter how much he lied to himself, his subconscious knew the truth and had determined that truth was going to come out, one way or the other.

Peter coughed, doing an admirable job of choking back his mirth. "Light and sweet."

"That makes two of us." Jordan pushed the buttons necessary to get the coffee. Armed with beverages, he turned to face Peter Alvarez and, he thought wryly, the truth.

"Thanks." Peter took the offered cup, then stepped back a half pace.

He's giving me room. Respecting my boundaries. Jordan didn't know if he should be disappointed or grateful.

"Maybe we should sit down and talk about what else we have in common." All humor had left Peter's expression.

Jordan had been able to avoid meeting Peter's gaze as he'd led him through the hangars and into the lounge. He had no excuse other than nerves to continue that ruse. So he met the other man's gaze and felt himself fall just a little.

"Yeah." Jordan exhaled heavily. "Maybe we should."

* * * *

"I would have been happy to throw together a meal," Tamara said as she scanned the menu. "I'm not used to eating out all that much."

Henry raised one eyebrow as he met his brother's gaze. "We have a better use for your energy in mind than cooking, Itty," he said.

"Well, I did enjoy the last meal we ate here. What are you guys going to have?"

"You can never go wrong if you choose the special," Morgan said.

"That's what I was thinking." Henry set his menu down. They were early for the dinner crowd, so the restaurant was only about half full. He'd been out of the country when Kelsey had come to Lusty and opened her restaurant. The first time he'd stepped into the place was after she'd already married his cousins. He'd have eaten here at least once a week out of family loyalty even if the food wasn't the best restaurant fare he'd ever had.

"The special was fried chicken, wasn't it?" Tamara closed her menu and set it down. "That does sound good. And since you do have a better use in mind for my energy that will probably be at least as vigorous as this afternoon's workout, I don't have to worry about the calories." She looked up, and Henry could see her gaze go to the front windows. "Hey, isn't that your brother?"

Since he had more than one, Henry turned to follow Tamara's gaze. Adam strolled down the sidewalk toward the restaurant. He wasn't surprised when Lusty's sheriff came in and headed straight for them.

"Ma'am, are these disreputable characters bothering you?" Adam greeted Tamara.

"No, they're harmless," she said.

"Hey, I take exception to being thought of as harmless," Henry said.

"Me, too," Morgan agreed. "Just wait until we get you home."

Adam chuckled as he pulled out the last chair at the table and made himself comfortable.

Henry met his gaze and got a bad feeling. He opened his mouth to object, but Adam shook his head.

Ginny Rose approached their table, carrying the tray of drinks—sweet tea—they'd ordered. Henry noticed her slight stumble when she saw Adam.

"Here you go," she said as she set the drinks down.

"Hello, Ginny."

No doubt about it, his brother's voice dipped to a gentler level when he addressed the waitress.

"Good afternoon, Sheriff."

When Adam continued to stare at her, she blushed, then said, "Adam." She cleared her throat. "Can I get you anything to drink?"

"Did you make the coffee?"

"Yes, I did. Just a few minutes ago."

"Then I'll have some of that, as you make a fine cup of coffee."

"Of course. I mean, thank you. I mean, um, I'll just go get it."

Henry thought if her face got any redder she might be in danger of having a stroke. He flicked a glance at Morgan and saw his brother was watching the interaction between their brother and the shy waitress with interest, too.

Adam's gaze followed Ginny as she went over to the beverage area. When she returned with his coffee, he thanked her, which only seemed to fluster the woman even more.

"If y'all are ready to order?"

They did, with Adam declining to order a meal but still watching her every move.

Henry thought Ginny's retreat to the kitchen could be characterized as an escape.

Adam turned his attention to Tamara. "Ms. Jones, do you mind if I ask you a couple of questions about the plane you flew into town in?"

Henry watched Tamara stiffen. "The Piper? I don't know if I can give you a lot of answers, Sheriff, as that plane and I hadn't been acquainted for long."

"How did you come to be flying it, then?"

"Damn it, Adam." Henry gave his brother as cold a stare as he could muster. There'd been a time when that look would have been enough to have his little brother backpedaling, fast.

Things had apparently changed more than Henry had realized in the years he'd been gone.

"You're the one who asked me to check out the plane. So back off and let me do my job."

Henry heard Tamara's gasp. "Because we thought someone was using her, and we wanted to know what the hell was going on," Henry said.

"You son of a bitch." Tamara's glare burned a hole in him. She pushed back her chair and would have stormed off. Adam's next words froze her in place.

"Sit down, Ms. Jones, or I'll arrest you and throw you in jail."

Henry had never heard that tone from Adam before. He met Morgan's gaze and knew he and his brother were only seconds away from pounding the hell out of the town sheriff, charges be damned.

"No one, including me, thinks you've done anything wrong. One thing you're going to have to learn, Tamara, is that Kendall men take care of what's theirs. That's why Henry asked me to run the plane. I ran you just because I figured these two Romeos weren't seeing beyond their swollen dicks."

"I *haven't* done anything wrong, and neither has my uncle! He bought the plane from a friend of his outside of Abilene."

"Yet you had no paperwork, and no flight plan filed for the jaunt," Adam said.

Henry sat back, the hardest thing he'd ever done, and let Tamara handle Adam. When she looked at him, he gave her what he hoped looked like an encouraging smile. Morgan reached over and laid his hand on her back.

"Uncle Goodwin said the paperwork was in transit. Mr. Smith told me I had to move the plane immediately, or he was going to have it demoed."

"And that didn't strike you as strange?" Adam asked.

Tamara sighed. She sat back and closed her eyes, and Henry understood that she had, that she'd been making excuses for the sloppy deal all the way around.

Tamara opened her eyes again and looked at Adam. "Yes, of course it did, but I'd put it down to being par for the course. My uncle has a habit of making…interesting friends. I just figured Smith was being a curmudgeon about things. So, what's up with the plane? It's stolen, isn't it?"

"It doesn't exist."

Henry sat forward. "What the hell do you mean, it doesn't exist?"

"I ran the registration numbers through the FAA and came up with nothing."

"So…maybe someone altered the numbers?" Tamara asked.

Adam didn't answer her. Instead he looked at Morgan and raised one eyebrow.

"More likely, is that record of the plane's existence has been expunged from the FAA's database." Morgan didn't sound happy about that fact, and Henry sure as hell wasn't pleased about it, either.

"What does that mean?" Tamara looked from Henry to Morgan and back again. Then she turned her attention back to Adam.

Henry knew Tamara was intuitive and smart. Her pique gone, she looked at each of them in turn again, but he could have sworn he saw her mind working.

"Nothing good," Adam said at last. "You might want to give your uncle a call."

"Is he in danger?"

Yes, she's smart as hell. "We won't let anything happen to him, sweetheart. Why don't you invite him down here for a visit?"

Tamara shook her head. "No. If there's danger, the last thing you need is for us to be here. Maybe I could—"

Morgan moved before Henry could. He reached over, turned Tamara's face to him, and gave her a fast, hard kiss. "Adam already told you, but let me repeat it, just so you have no doubt. You belong to us, and we Kendalls take care of our own."

"Damn right." Henry looked over at Adam. "We need to get that man here, as soon as possible."

"That's why I wanted Tamara to give him a call. Let him know I'm on my way."

Tamara looked at Morgan and then him. "Bossy. The two of you are a couple of bossy, dominating, Alpha *dogs*."

"It's a good thing you realize that, sweetheart," Morgan said.

"It will save a lot of time and grief in the years to come," Henry added.

Tamara grabbed her hair and screamed. "Argh!"

"You know, she sounded exactly like Mom just now," Adam said.

Henry tried not to laugh, but it was tough. The truth was there were more than a couple of passing similarities between their woman and their mother.

He thought it would probably be wise, however, to avoid pointing them out to Tamara at the moment.

Chapter 14

Tamara paced the front porch of the Kendall family home—the New House as it was called. Unable to sit down or relax, the pacing helped to keep her calm. She reminded herself that Uncle Goodwin was safe, and that was all that really mattered. He was with Adam Kendall, and the two of them should be arriving soon.

She still didn't feel right about accepting the Kendalls' hospitality, under the circumstances. Letting others come under fire because of wrong choices was how her parents handled things. It wasn't her way, nor was it Goodwin's. Yet he had readily accepted the family's invitation to stay with them.

If there'd been a ground-floor bedroom at the cottage, she'd have insisted he stay with her. But there wasn't, and since he could no longer navigate stairs all that well, his staying here made perfect sense.

It made sense, but Tamara was surprised it was actually going to happen. Hell, she'd been shocked that he'd so quickly agreed to accompany the sheriff back to Lusty in the first place.

She'd always believed her uncle to be as fiercely independent as she herself had always been.

After speaking with Goodwin earlier, Tamara was more convinced than ever there had to be something wonky about the business surrounding the Piper.

Her uncle had admitted to not really knowing John Smith all that well. He'd confessed that since the moment she'd called him after the plane had malfunctioned, he'd been trying to get in touch with the man, but with no success.

John Smith wasn't answering his e-mails or his phone. Not only that, but the promised documents for the Piper had never turned up.

"Here, Tamara."

Tamara turned at the sound of the feminine voice. She hadn't heard Samantha Kendall come out onto the porch. The older woman held out a glass, and Tamara took it.

"A tiny bit of brandy," Samantha said. "It will help settle your nerves."

"How can you be so kind to me when I'm putting your entire family in danger?"

"You're doing no such thing. I agree there are suspicious circumstances surrounding the plane that brought you here. But I have every faith we'll figure it all out, just as I have faith in the men of this family to keep us all safe."

Tamara shook her head. "We both know there's a lot of crime going on in this part of the country. That plane could have been involved in anything—drug smuggling, human trafficking, the dealing of illegal weapons—"

Henry and Morgan both came out of the house onto the porch.

"Itty Bitty, that plane is as tiny as you are," Henry said. "No big crime syndicate is likely to have used it, as it doesn't have much of a cargo capacity."

"Probably we're erring on the side of caution," Morgan said. "Maybe there's a very good reason the plane isn't registered. I've made a couple of inquiries with some people I know. We should have some answers soon. In the meantime, we make sure both you and your uncle are here and safe. It's just prudence, is all."

Despite everything, Tamara felt herself smile. "You have a way of making the most extraordinary situation sound perfectly normal. Just what was it you did in the Air Force, Morgan?"

"Oh, a little of this and a little of that." Morgan grinned.

Tamara wondered just what it was Morgan was trying to tell her. "That's not very definitive. Were you involved in black ops?"

"The Air Force doesn't have black ops," Morgan said. "Just ask anyone."

"No, of course they don't." Tamara would have said something more, but the sound of a car coming down the lane stopped her.

The sheriff's car pulled to a stop at the head of the driveway, not far from the porch. Tamara wasted no time running down the steps. She reached the car in time to open the front passenger door.

"Well now just hold your horses, girl, I'm getting out." Goodwin Hornsby placed one weathered hand on the top of the open door and levered himself out of the car.

He matched her in height, though she suspected that in his prime he'd been a little bit taller. His small frame probably held a good thirty pounds more than it should, but he didn't seem overweight to her. He could no longer move as spryly as when she first came to him, but his stamina still nearly matched her own. The only outward clues to his age were the snow-white cap of hair on his head, and the fact that he could predict weather according to the bursitis in his joints.

Goodwin Hornsby, God bless him, would never see seventy-five again.

Tamara didn't know why she felt so sentimental all of a sudden. But she did, so she threw her arms around the only person who—until very recently—had given one good damn about her in her entire life.

"There, now." He patted her shoulder, an awkward movement for him, she thought, since she'd so rarely clung to him. "Best let me free so I can go and greet my hosts."

Tamara stepped back. She met his gaze, the light in those so-familiar eyes intelligent and fierce.

"I know you," he said. "You're feeling prickly and have your nose out of joint on account of you can't handle this situation all on your own. It's not weakness to accept help when it's needed, Tamara Jones."

Tamara looked up at the people waiting on the porch, then back at her uncle. "Some habits are hard to break, Uncle Goodwin."

"Well, I reckon there're worse ones a body could be saddled with." He turned and nodded to Adam, who still stood by the driver's door. "Thank you, Sheriff. I appreciate the ride."

"You're welcome, Mr. Hornsby."

Goodwin turned to take in the people on the porch. Tamara followed his gaze and noted that practically every member of the Kendall family had come out to greet him.

He walked in the way he did when his joints were hurting him. Tamara ached to help him, but she knew better. Goodwin Hornsby might say she needed to learn to be gracious and take a helping hand from time to time, but he sure as hell didn't apply that advice to himself very often.

He gained the top of the porch and nodded at the senior brothers Kendall, speaking before she had the chance to introduce him. "I knew your mother. Miranda Kendall was a fine teacher. She taught me a darn sight more than just reading and spelling. I came to her class an untamed boy, and she taught me how to focus my mind and how to think."

Preston smiled. "Mother used to brag that she'd had a hand in shaping that sharp business brain of yours, Mr. Hornsby. Welcome to our home."

"Thank you. And thank you for looking out for my girl, here."

"You don't need to thank us for that," Morgan said.

Morgan stood beside her and set his hand on her right shoulder. She felt Henry approach on her left side. Having them both there made her feel secure.

"Yes, I see that," Goodwin said. "Well, good then."

It wasn't the men's proprietary conduct or her uncle's accepting attitude that commanded all of Tamara's attention.

She looked at the fathers. "You know my uncle?"

"Before today, we've never had the pleasure of meeting him. But of course, he's a very well-known man in the world of business and finance in Texas," Charles said. "Dozens of thriving, successful businesses in the state owe their success to Goodwin Hornsby." He tilted his head slightly as he said that. Then he glanced at his brothers. The senior Kendalls all appeared as bewildered as she felt.

Tamara looked at her uncle. "How come I've never known this?"

"Well now." Goodwin met her gaze straight-on. "You came to me a mite beat up by life and those that should have had a proper care for you. What they'd done to you, it more or less warped your perception of people. Always figured there'd come a day when you'd be able to see a bit more clearly."

His answer, given kindly enough, still stung.

"I've just made a fresh pot of coffee, Mr. Hornsby. Won't you please come in?" Samantha Kendall stepped forward and placed a hand on Goodwin's arm.

"Thank you. Coffee sounds good."

Tamara stood back as her uncle, accompanied by most of the Kendall family, trooped into the house. The sound of conversation reached her, telling her they were already on the road to becoming good friends.

Morgan and Henry stayed with her, and that shouldn't have surprised her, but it did. She had the sense that somehow, over the past couple of days, her life had completely changed.

"Do you want to go inside, join the party?"

Morgan's question, quietly asked, told her that if she said no, they'd go with her wherever she wanted to go.

She looked from one to the other of these two very charismatic and sexy flyboys. What she wanted to do was go back to the cottage and just be with them. She had a feeling they knew that, too.

Tamara inhaled deeply then smiled. That would come later. Right now, her uncle was inside this house, having a good time already by the sounds of it. And that's where she wanted to be, too.

"Yeah. Let's go in for a while. Then we can go back to the cottage."

Morgan slipped his arm around her and gave her a quick kiss. Then he linked the fingers of his left hand with her right.

Henry took her other hand. For all of the passion they'd shared so far, they'd only both of them held her hands at the same time once before.

Tamara didn't really know what turn her life had taken in the last few days. Not knowing was the same as not being in control, and that was a state she usually avoided at all costs. It did surprise her that she found this simple custom, having her hands clasped by these two men, to be a gesture that steadied her. Steadied, she knew she could reason it all out later.

Tamara nodded and accompanied them into the house.

* * * *

They'd left a light burning on the porch. The sight of it, and the house, filled Tamara with a kind of warmth she never expected to experience. It felt like coming home.

Get that silly notion out of your head right now, Tamara Jones.

She had a home, approximately a hundred miles due south, and she'd do well to remember that. All through the evening at the Kendalls' she'd felt different. She'd been a part of that large crowd, seated around the enormous dining room table, listening to stories, telling a few herself, partaking of what she understood was called "family." She'd had fun in a way she'd never imagined she would. The most amazing thing was that she hadn't felt like an outsider. She'd felt as if she belonged to that group and with those people.

That doesn't make Lusty, Texas, home.

"When do you think we'll know something? About that damn plane?" Tamara might have regretted the churlish tone, but her companions simply smiled at her and acted as if they hadn't heard it.

"Don't curse that plane, Itty. It brought you to us." Henry's smile worked like magic to soothe her mood. He hefted the suitcase her uncle had so thoughtfully packed for her and kept a hand at her elbow—gentlemanly courtesy—as they mounted the steps.

"It could be a few days," Morgan said. "I've not been retired that long, but neither do I have the clearance I once had. We'll have to wait and see if any of my contacts will respond to my inquiry."

"You were a Captain, Henry was a Colonel, and yet you had the higher security clearance. Yeah, right, no black ops in the Air Force." Tamara grinned. Morgan leaned over and kissed her. Then he straightened and unlocked the door.

"Until we know what's what, we'll just carry on as usual," he said.

They didn't bother to turn on any of the downstairs lights. Instead, they just headed for the second story.

Henry set the suitcase beside the bed. "What will it be, Tamara? Shower, bath, or Jacuzzi?"

"Decisions, decisions." She shouldn't be all that interested in getting naked with these men so soon after the sex fest they'd indulged in for most of the day.

She shouldn't, but in truth there was nothing she wanted to do more.

"Shower, please."

Good choice, Tamara thought a few minutes later. The scented steam enveloped her, and soapy, masculine hands caressed her. Over, around, down, and between those knowledgeable fingers cleansed, yes, but they also teased and promised and aroused.

"Lock your fingers together around my neck, Red." Morgan's husky whisper from behind tickled her ear and heated her blood.

She did as he asked, and the new position brought his cock closer, to rub against her back and entice her bottom. His hands swept over her stomach, then down, his fingers touching and tantalizing her slit, making her wet, making her burn.

Standing in front of her, Henry soaped his hands again and spread them over her breasts, cupping, smoothing, and plucking. Tamara sighed as the velvety strokes turned her nipples even harder.

"Your breasts are so wonderfully responsive to us, sweetheart," Henry said. He leaned forward and kissed her, a light and playful kiss that ended way too soon. She smiled despite being denied a deeper taste of him.

"Her pussy likes us, too," Morgan said.

"Mm, it sure does," Tamara agreed. "Speaking of responsiveness, there're a couple of cocks real close by that seem awfully happy to see me."

"They aren't just happy to see you, Red, they're eager to fuck you," Morgan said. He nipped her ear. "I want to fuck your ass. Will you let me?"

The dark and forbidden request sent tiny shards of excitement skittering across her skin and down deep to pool in her stomach. Her nipples clenched to an almost painful rigidity. Tamara didn't know how long this conflagration between them would burn, but while it did, she wanted every thrill she could grab.

"Yes. Yes, I want you to fuck my ass."

"Good." Morgan trailed the fingers of one hand up and down the crack of her ass, using the slide of soap to arouse her. When one finger circled the rosette of her anus, she moaned, because the shivery sensations shot her arousal higher and made her hunger for more.

"You're responsive here, too, baby," Morgan said. "I think your entire body knows it belongs to us."

Tamara refused to comment or even to think about such an outrageous statement. Certainly, these two flyboys turned her on completely. What they shared was exciting and hot. But she, more than most, understood how fleeting attraction and affection could be.

Fortunately, it didn't seem either man expected a response to Morgan's claim. Tamara pushed that heavy thought away. She wanted to focus on the moment.

Together Morgan and Henry rinsed her, and together they gently toweled her dry. Morgan scooped her into his arms and carried her to the bed. He stood her on her feet and cupped her face between his hands. His kiss felt tender, nearly reverent, and Tamara wondered about that, about his ability to be gentle when she knew he shook with need.

He drew back and brushed her bottom lip with his thumb. "Middle of the bed, sweetheart, on your hands and knees."

Why did this position make her feel so wicked, wild, and wanton? Tamara's senses had come acutely alive. Though not voluptuous, her breasts hung, swaying slightly with each tiny movement of her hips, the motion feeling sensuous. Her bottom, naked and vulnerable, pushed up toward her lover, an offering given freely.

Morgan reached out, stroked her ass, and she shivered in anticipation. He crawled onto the bed behind her and placed kisses on her flesh, trailing them up her spine.

Tented by his body, she felt the heat of him seep down deep into her, warming every atom, every nerve. When he pressed closer and rubbed his engorged cock against her, she moaned.

"Don't tease me." She'd gotten very hot very quickly. She'd learned to like drawing things out and playing in the last couple of days. But right then, she just wanted the payoff.

"Not teasing, baby. Just give me a moment to prepare us both."

She looked over her shoulder as Morgan rolled on the condom. His brother handed him a tub of lube, and he generously coated two fingers.

"Tamara."

Henry stretched out beside her and stroked her, gently brushing the sides of her breasts. When she turned her face toward him, he kissed her, his lips wet and hot, mating perfectly with hers. His tongue stroked deeply into her mouth at the same time Morgan's fingers stroked her anus, spreading the lubricant, getting her ready for his cock.

When he inserted a finger into her, she shivered and pushed her ass closer to him.

Henry ended the kiss. "It's such a turn-on, the way you want us."

She met his gaze but let her eyes drift shut when Morgan moved his finger in and out of her anus.

"Easy." Morgan moved, and Tamara felt the heat of his latex-covered cock pressing against her. He was so hot, and so much bigger than the butt plug they'd used.

"I'll stop if you tell me to, Tamara. Always."

"Please, fuck me." She felt desperate to have him in her this way.

His hands on the globes of her ass spread her cheeks. And then she felt him press forward. Pressure built, a burning kind of pressure as her anus stretched, oh so slowly giving way. The burning grew, edged to pain, a hungry kind of pain that demanded surrender, that promised unimagined bliss.

Tamara whimpered, and Morgan froze. "Do you want me to stop?"

"No. I need...oh, God, I don't know what I need. More."

"Shh. Let me do this gently, Red. I don't want to hurt you."

Arousal became a jungle cat, clawing to get out. "I don't care."

"Well, I sure as hell do."

Tamara pushed back, and Morgan hissed.

Henry moved beside her, and then she felt his fingers stroking her clit. She began to shiver as if being zapped by a dozen little electrodes.

The pain of Morgan's invasion turned into a white-hot energy, charging her blood and her nerve endings with such exquisite need. She felt her pussy grow impossibly wet, and she could only push back, a nonverbal plea for more.

"God, yes." Morgan's cock slid all the way in, a slow, deep penetration that held her in a frenzied grip of pre-orgasmic bliss. "Hold still, baby. Give your body a moment to stretch."

Tamara couldn't, and she couldn't help it. She began to move her hips, the need to come visceral.

"Damn." Morgan shuddered. Then he pulled his cock out, and slid it back again. Once more he withdrew, his fingers gripping her ass hard, then pushed into her again. He did it again, and then again, each thrust measured but fierce, his entire body shaking with his effort to stay in control.

Tamara's climax raced toward her, huge, relentless, wave after wave of rapture that drenched her and filled her, rapture that stole her breath and her heart and her reason. On and on, deeper and brighter, Tamara prayed the pleasure would never end, even as she wondered how she could ever survive it.

Chapter 15

"Damn it all to hell. I'm always one *fucking* step behind that fucking plane!" Preston bent down, scooped a loose rock off the ground, and heaved it at the pickup truck parked nearby.

The resulting *ping* didn't make him feel a whole lot better. Dennis, the owner of the truck, proved he was smarter than Preston had given him credit for being. He kept his mouth shut and waited.

Preston paced away, down the shoulder of the road, away from his own car and driver, away from his men.

Jesus Christ, if I don't find that plane soon, that bastard Ramos is going to have me killed. Preston had no doubt whatsoever of that. He was running out of time and, it looked like, running out of options.

For a long moment he let his gaze drift over the central Texas landscape. This state road, not as busy as the Interstate, still seemed to be busy enough. Preston thought it might be a good idea to get moving. No sense just standing around taking the chance they'd be noticed and reported.

He headed back toward his men. "There's an IHOP listed at the second exit off I-35. Let's head for it. Dennis, I want you to ride with me and let Jimmy drive your truck."

"Sure thing, boss."

Dennis got in the backseat with him. Lorne swung the Buick around, heading away from the small ranch owned by one G. Hornsby, and back toward the Interstate.

"Okay, tell me everything again," Preston said.

"I did as you ordered, and drove back and forth past the house, and then took a tour around the area. I stopped at the Gas 'N' Go because it's only a couple of miles from Hornsby's place, and I figured he might be known there. Hornsby has an old Jeep parked at the side of the garage, looks like it's been there for a while. So I pretended I was interested in buying it, asked if the store owner knew the guy."

Preston nodded. Dennis *was* smarter than he'd originally thought. "That was good thinking."

"Yeah, well, the store clerk knew Hornsby's name well enough but had no idea where the man could have gone. Mentioned he lived with his niece, that it was just the two of them. As we were talking, another customer came in and overheard us. He claimed Hornsby was away for at least the next few days. Said he'd spoken to him just before he rode off in a sheriff's cruiser. He told the store owner how he'd thought it must have been a joke because of the name on the side of the cruiser, and that maybe Hornsby was on his way to pull some kind of prank on someone. But the store owner said no, there really was such a place."

"Such a place as where?"

"Lusty, Texas. That's what the guy who came into the store said was on the sheriff's car. He'd thought Hornsby was pulling a prank on his niece by showing up in a phony sheriff's department car, because that's who he said he was going to go join, his niece."

"Lusty, Texas." Preston had never heard of the place. "We'll get Jimmy to look it up on the Web, see what we can find out about the place."

"Well anyway, when I heard that, I decided not to go back to the man's house and break in. If he's connected to cops, they might be keeping an eye on his property while he's gone, or something."

Preston looked over at Dennis. "I agree. We can't take a chance, at least not during daylight. But I do want you to go on foot onto the property tonight, have a look in that barn. It's big enough to hold a Piper."

"Yes, sir."

They arrived at the IHOP a few minutes later. As with most eateries found at the end of an Interstate off-ramp, the place was busy for mid-morning, but not stand-in-line crowded. They grabbed a table in the back, ordered only coffee.

Preston sat beside Jimmy, who got his laptop working, searching out information on Lusty, Texas.

"They've got a Web site," Jimmy said quietly. "Looking at the map, I'd say it's about a hundred miles north. Doesn't appear to have a direct Interstate ramp. Incorporated as a town in the 1880s. They do have a sheriff's department, but that agency doesn't have a separate Web site, so it can't be very big, or very up to date. Yeah, population's only a couple of thousand people."

"So why would the sheriff of a pissant Texas town come all the way to San Marcos to pick up Hornsby? You figure he's been arrested?" Preston asked.

Dennis shook his head. "That's what the store guy asked the other guy. He said, no, Hornsby and the sheriff seemed real friendly-like. Hornsby sat in the front, which he wouldn't have been doing if he'd been under arrest."

Jimmy had stilled and looked over at Preston, a smile on his face.

"What?"

"They have an airstrip. It's only a small, private airfield, but it's capable of handling small jets. It's cross-referenced on an FAA list."

Preston looked down at the information Jimmy had up on the screen. "Show me the map again." When his man complied, he said, "Can you pull back, so I can see a larger...yeah, like that. Look, this Lusty is about halfway between Abilene and San Marcos. Maybe whoever was flying that Piper had trouble and had to set it down?"

"Let me search for any small plane crashes," Jimmy said.

His fingers flew over the keyboard. "No, there's nothing. So we know it didn't crash."

"Good damn thing or we'd all be in a world of hurt right now," Preston said.

He looked up at his men. "Okay, here's what we're going to do. We'll grab a couple of rooms over there at the Barn Swallow Inn. Tonight, when it's dark, Dennis and you will go have a look around Hornsby's place. See if the Piper's there. At this point we don't know that it's not. If it's not, tomorrow we head to Lusty. Check out the airstrip. I'll come up with some sort of a story, as we'll likely be dealing with more than one person."

While his men nodded their understanding, Preston stepped back, mentally, and looked at the big picture. Tomorrow would tell the tale. He either found that plane and retrieved Miguel Ramos' property, or one way or another, he disappeared.

* * * *

"Looks like quite the addition you're building here," Goodwin said.

Morgan stood beside Tamara's uncle as he looked around the airfield. This morning, Jordan not only had himself and Peter Alvarez hard at work on the hangar, but several and various Kendall, Jessop, and Benedict cousins as well.

"It's got to be big enough for at least two planes for our new flight service, plus room to restore vintage aircraft, which we both want to take up as a hobby. Also, there needs to be room to house the Investigation agency—and it seemed prudent to make room for a couple more businesses, for the future. Our brother Jordan is a general contractor, which has been handy for us. We're hoping to be finished by the end of the month."

"Had planned to operate our two-man crop-dusting operation out of a small airfield about ten miles from our place outside of San Marcos," Goodwin said, looking directly at him. "Of course, this location would work better, if you were thinking of a long-term merger."

Morgan felt the weight of Goodwin Hornsby's shrewd assessment. He didn't pretend not to know what the man was talking about.

This part of the conversation was likely why the man had invited himself along this morning in the first place. "Henry and I were decided on that merger the first day we met Tamara. She, on the other hand, is going to need time to be convinced. She sure as hell doesn't trust easily, and she doesn't expect our relationship to last."

"You know her well already, I see." Goodwin Hornsby shook his head and looked off to the south for a moment. Then he turned his head and met Morgan's gaze. "Yep, I lay the blame for that at the feet of her parents. My opinion? Just because a body can birth children doesn't automatically mean they should."

"Amen to that."

"I never broadcast my means among the family, on account of too many of 'em were born leeches—like Tamara's mother, Mary-Ellen. You might say, in some respects, our gene pool had no lifeguard."

Morgan's laughter burst from him while Goodwin nodded and gave him an almost shy smile.

"Anyway, it wasn't hard over the years to keep mum, as my relatives tended to write me off as being strange, which in turn made them keep their distance. I never sought the spotlight in life, either. I'm not that well known outside of certain business circles."

"I think Tamara is pissed with herself for making assumptions where you're concerned," Morgan said.

"Well, she shouldn't be. You might say I deliberately deceived her, at least in the beginning. You have to remember, when she first came to me, I didn't know what was going on with her. But she was kin, so of course I took her in. When I realized she'd come to me as a last-ditch cry for help, why, then I focused on providing her something she'd never had, a stable home environment. Suited me fine, having her accept me just because of my being me, and not because of my bank account. Still, I'll make it right with her."

Morgan led the way to where the grounded Piper waited for repairs. He remained quiet while Goodwin walked over to the plane then slowly examined it.

"What do you think the story is here?" he asked.

"I don't have a clue," Although he had his suspicions, and no matter which way he looked at it, the picture wasn't good. "The fact that the plane isn't on any FAA list stinks of agency manipulation. Which agency, I can't say. Hopefully, we'll have some answers soon."

"Do you really believe there's a danger to Tamara or myself?"

Morgan spread his hands. "I've learned to be careful and to listen to my gut. I hope I'm wrong."

"I've had amazing luck in business in my heyday, and more recently on the Web, both professionally, and personally. I have to tell you, that plane not being listed, that doesn't bother me. My being unable to get hold of Smith? *That* bothers me. Your brother said he'd reach out to the state police, have them do some checking on the man. It occurs to me if we're in danger, he could be, too."

"True. But it started with him. If he's in danger, it could be because he sold something he didn't have a right to sell." Morgan put his hands in his pockets and leaned against the door. "What's *your* gut telling you?"

"That despite the background check I did, I've been taken for a ride. I imagine the money I wired to the man to pay for this here Piper is lost, and as I agree with you, he likely didn't have the right to sell the damn thing to me in the first place. I imagine someone's going to show up with the papers to prove it. Eighty thousand down the drain, but that's my own stupid fault. My mistake, so I can pay that price. But if my actions have put Tamara in danger, well, that's a price I'm not willing to pay."

"She landed it like a pro," Morgan said. "And now she belongs to us, and you can bet your ass we're going to keep her safe."

Goodwin met his gaze, and Morgan saw there was a hell of a lot of intelligence and determination in those eyes.

"No," Goodwin Hornsby said, then came over and gave Morgan a pat on the shoulder. "I'm not betting my ass, son. I'm betting yours. Yours and your brother's."

Morgan nodded. "Understood."

They headed back to the construction site. Morgan intended to see Goodwin off in the car he'd been loaned by one of his fathers and then get back to work. Otherwise, the rest of the family would razz him about being a slacker.

Just a few dozen feet from where Tamara's uncle had parked the car, Morgan stopped. As usual, his gaze sought out his woman. He found her instantly—and recognized the petite white-haired woman she was chatting with.

Apparently Goodwin recognized her, too.

"Well, Kate Benedict!" He made his way over to the women.

"Goodwin Hornsby! When Samantha called me this morning I knew I had to make my way here as soon as possible." Kate gave the older man a hug and sent Morgan what he could only call a sly wink.

Tamara and Henry came over to join them. She came to stand close to him, and he recognized the look of shock on her face. Kate Benedict could take some getting used to.

"I've been busy this week with the last-minute arrangements for my granddaughter's ceremony," Kate said, stepping back from Goodwin, making the group into a kind of circle. "But I've been meaning to come over and meet Tamara, here."

"When my girl called me to tell me she'd made an emergency landing right here in Lusty, I of course thought of you and Gerald and Patrick. It's been a lot of years, woman."

"My, yes it has been! And imagine that, Tamara just…falling out of the sky as it were, landing almost at Morgan and Henry's feet!"

The laughter in Grandma Kate's eyes was impossible to resist, so Morgan didn't even try. "Yes," Morgan said to her. "Imagine that."

"Now, I understand that you're both going to be here tomorrow, so of course you must come to the ceremony. And before either of you thinks to argue, I know that Susan, Colt, and Ryder would be thrilled to have you there." She touched Morgan's arm. "I'm so glad that you and Henry decided to stay in Lusty and open this new business here." Then she beamed a huge smile at Tamara's uncle. "The party tomorrow is going to be a real celebration!"

"I wouldn't miss it," Goodwin said.

Kate turned her raised-eyebrow look on Tamara. "What about you, Tamara? Will I see you there, too?"

His woman's smile in return proved what Morgan had always known. There wasn't a person on God's green earth who could resist Kate Benedict.

"I'd already planned to attend," Tamara said.

"Now that's just perfect. Well, if you'll excuse me, I'm off to go have a cup of tea over at Kelsey's restaurant. If I time it right, Ginny Rose will be on her break."

Tamara looked confused. "You don't want her to wait on you?"

"No, I don't. I want her to *join* me. Did you know that Adam and Jake are sweet on her? And who could blame them, really? *I* certainly like her." Kate gave a quick wave to all of them—including those who'd been working away while she'd visited, and then headed for her car.

The woman could walk faster than he did, and that was saying something. Morgan shook his head and then looked over at Henry.

"You see?" his brother said. "I told you we didn't have anything to worry about."

"Pardon me, but I'm confused." Tamara looked up at Morgan, clearly wanting him to straighten out her confusion. "*That* is the woman you asked me if I knew just after we met, isn't it?"

"I'll explain it all later, Red."

"Well, if you'll excuse me, I've been invited by your fathers to go over to the Big House with them. Something about looking over the partnership agreement for that Investigative agency the Benedicts are setting up."

"Well, good," Henry said. "That means we won't have to worry about keeping our uncles off any of the ladders, at least not today."

"Aw, could be they just want to feel they're a part of their own business, hit the ground running, as it were. I sure know how that feels," Goodwin said.

"That's the part about our uncles on the ladders that we're worried about," Morgan said. "The part that involves them hitting the ground."

Chapter 16

"So what you're telling me is that Kate Benedict *picked* you out for her grandsons?" Tamara couldn't keep the incredulity out of her voice.

The woman standing before her was a vision. Hair so black it nearly sparkled blue in the Texas sun, eyes of startling violet, she looked like the sort of woman who'd have men lined up out the door and down the block.

"I suppose that sounds kind of funny, doesn't it? Actually I guess you could say that Grandma Kate didn't so much pick me out for them as she simply facilitated my meeting them, as she thought we belonged together. And really, that's all she did—um, well, until she had us stranded in the middle of nowhere, that is."

"Hey, geek boy, quit staring at your woman and get back to work!" Jordan's shout carried throughout the entire airfield, Tamara was certain of it.

"You're just jealous, there, Bob the Builder, 'cause you don't have a love life of your own at the moment!" Joshua Benedict's rebuttal sounded just as loud.

"Boys." Penelope sighed the one word that said so much and shook her head. "They all get together, and I swear, no matter what it is they're doing, the maturity level drops at least fifteen years."

"I think it has to do with that Y chromosome thing they have going on there," Tamara said. Then she laughed. "At least now I understand a little about why Morgan asked me if I knew Kate Benedict just moments after he tackled me to the ground. Which, of course, I didn't until earlier today. She seemed like such a sweet, if very energetic, lady."

"I love her, but then I've known her for years. The entire family—Benedicts, Kendalls, and Jessops alike—are watching her nervously, wondering who it is she's going to set her matchmaking sights on next," Penelope agreed. "But that isn't why he would have asked you that, exactly. It's what Kate said to him when he told her, very politely, I might add, that he and Henry didn't need her help finding a wife."

Tamara blinked. "Hey, I'm not wife material. I'm just here until we solve the mystery surrounding that Piper I flew in on." Tamara told the truth. Sure, she might be enjoying the best sex of her life, finally discovering that she was a sensual woman, after all. That didn't mean marriage was on the table, or anywhere near it.

She was brought back to the conversation by the twinkle in Penelope's eye. The other woman tilted her head to the side. "Don't you want to know the punch line?"

Tamara was about to ask Penelope to explain her cryptic comment when a car turned off the state road and headed for the front of the older hangars.

"Anyone expecting someone in a dark blue Buick Regal?" Jordan asked from his perch on the top of the hangar. Being the only professional builder on the site, he'd staked out the highest and most dangerous position for himself.

When no one answered him, Morgan said, "Crap, tourists. I'll get rid of them."

"Tourists?" Tamara asked.

"Yeah, we get some every once in a while. They see it's an airfield, and they wonder if they can rent a plane, or take lessons, stuff like that."

"Which they will be able to do, soon," she said.

"Well, true enough. But that's soon, not now, damn it."

"Don't scare off potential customers," Henry called after him.

Morgan, who'd just gotten down off a ladder and was heading toward her, waved his hand in the air in response to his brother's taunt. He stopped beside Tamara and swooped in for a kiss.

She couldn't help but respond to the heat of his mouth or the seduction of his tongue. She opened wide, sucked him in, and let her own tongue dance with his. His flavor drenched her and fired her blood, making her instantly crave him. She wished the three of them were back at the cottage, naked and stretched out on that gloriously decadent bed.

As quickly as he'd bent to her, he straightened again and headed for the door to the helicopter hangar.

"Once the family finds out about this, they are going to be *seriously* freaked," Penelope said. "Any single men and women not wishing to be matched at this time will likely go on sudden, impromptu, and extended vacations."

Tamara shook her head and looked at the woman she'd thought to be as intelligent and logical as she was beautiful.

"Um, because Morgan Kendall kissed me? It was, to quote the title of a really good book I read not that long ago, *Just A Kiss*."

"When Morgan said he and Henry would find their own woman when the time was right, Kate said, and I quote, 'You say that as if the right woman is going to just fall right out of the sky,' end quote." Penelope's grin widened.

Tamara opened her mouth and then snapped it shut again. Then she shook her head. "I may have 'fallen' out of the sky, but trust me, I am not the right woman, and this is not a forever kind of thing happening here between us. Forever may be good for some people, and more power to them. But some of us just don't have the stick-to-itiveness gene in our makeup."

Penelope didn't argue the matter, which won her points in Tamara's opinion. So much so that she decided to forgive the small look of pity the other woman sent her. Penelope Primrose was a woman in love, and everyone knew women in love wanted to spread what they considered the happy condition to all and sundry.

Tamara had seen what love looked like, Jones-style. She'd seen it in the desperation on her mother's face when her latest boyfriend took a walk, and in the way her father kept trying to make himself younger and more hip for each successive, younger girlfriend.

Love had made her parents into selfish, hard individuals who easily forgot they had a daughter between them.

No, Tamara Jones had seen love up close and personal, and she wanted no part of it. She nodded her head once for emphasis, even while her right hand moved up to massage the tiny ache that bloomed deep in her chest.

* * * *

Morgan strolled through the helicopter hangar, hands in pockets, his focus on appearing relaxed and at ease. Henry was right, it wouldn't do to scare off any potential customers, which the person or persons in the Buick could very well be.

Morgan wasn't known for being overly loquacious, or friendly. That was Henry's talent and he had no doubt that, given complete freedom, his brother would build their business clientele in record time.

The dark blue Buick sat, motor turned off, just to the left of the Lear hangar. Morgan frowned. The large bay door to that hangar stood wide open, likely, he knew, because they'd all hit the drink machines and the lounge around lunchtime. This hangar had the best bathroom facilities, too, which would have accounted for the door being left up.

Just inside a man stood, his back ramrod straight. Going with his gut impression, Morgan thought he carried himself like a man whose senses had been turned on high alert. The man's beige chinos, brown loafers and blue sport coat told Morgan this wasn't one of the area's rough-and-tumble ranchers. Yet he didn't think the label "tourist" fit him, either.

"May I help you?"

The stranger pivoted neatly, his eyes landing on Morgan then skittering off to either side, and Morgan felt his own body go on alert. When the stranger smiled, the light of that smile didn't reach his eyes.

Grandma Kate had once told him to be wary of people whose smile didn't reach their eyes.

"Oh, hi there. I didn't know this was here, you know? I just happened to look over as I was driving and said to myself, hey, that's an airport."

"This airfield has been here for several years." Morgan couldn't put his finger on what it was about the man that set him off. He decided to play the role of taciturn local.

"Well, yeah, I guess it has been, when you think about it. Finding it here was a surprise."

Morgan simply raised one eyebrow and waited.

"The name's Rogers. Preston Rogers. I'd like to hire you to fly me to New York City. I have a business meeting at the beginning of December, and I thought, you know, this would be a lot better than flying commercial. And hey, I'd be willing to pay top rate."

"I'm sorry, this is a private airfield. The planes here aren't for hire."

"Oh." Rogers turned back and appeared to be giving the Learjet a covetous glance. "That's too bad." Then he laughed. "I was just noticing your planes. They're kind of like aviation's version of the odd couple, don't you think? One twin-engine jet, the other a single-engine Piper."

The man must know his planes. The Piper didn't have a label on it. Morgan filed that bit of information away. "They're not my planes. Like I said, this is a private airfield."

"Oh. Yes, you did say that. Okay, then. I'm sorry to have bothered you."

Morgan watched as the man took his time, ambled to his car. He seemed to be simply enjoying the scenery as he walked. The airfield was on a pretty piece of land. Or, Morgan thought, he could be conducting surveillance, casing the joint.

Rogers started his car, then backed up cautiously, before swinging the wheel around and heading back to the state road. The man drove his car like he had all the time in the world.

Morgan stood for a moment, his hands still in his pockets, and tried to figure out what his gut was telling him.

"Trouble?"

He looked over as another relative stranger stood just a few feet away from him, looking at him with a cool, assessing stare.

"I'm not sure."

He didn't know how much information Jordan had shared with Peter Alvarez about the circumstances surrounding the Piper. Personally, his instincts told him to just keep all his cards close to the vest for the time being.

Peter shrugged and walked past him, over to the glass enclosed lounge, making a beeline for the soda machine.

"Get you one?" he asked.

"No. Thank you."

"There was some good-hearted speculation that the tourist would be sent packing in such a way that he'd likely never darken the doorstep again—evidenced, it was decided, by the car fishtailing as it sped off for parts unknown and safety. And I should also confess that money was involved in this speculation."

Morgan laughed. "My family doesn't seem to have much faith in my ability to be polite and circumspect when the situation warrants."

"Well, I don't know you. *I* bet you'd be just that. You sure I can't buy you a can of soda? I kind of feel as if I owe you, since I was the only one who took that bet."

"You bet against Jordan?" Since there was nothing more to be done with regard to the recently departed Preston Rogers, Morgan turned his attention to Peter Alvarez. Morgan took the few steps necessary to bring him to the lounge. He'd only spoken to Peter one time. It seemed a good opportunity to conduct a subtle interrogation.

Peter shrugged. He fed some coins into the dispenser. The sound of a can dropping echoed loudly in the cavernous hangar. "Jordan isn't temperamental," he said. He scooped his can, opened it, and took a good long drink.

"You seem to know him pretty well on such short acquaintance." Morgan wasn't sure how he felt about that.

"I wouldn't say I know him that well," Peter said. "I've simply paid attention."

"Are you trying to placate me?"

Peter gave him a level look. "No, I'm trying to be honest. You're his brother, and you're important to him. And I understand your desire to protect him. I'm not a threat, not to him, and not to you."

Damned if Morgan didn't feel just like a heavy-handed older sibling. Of course, he couldn't help it. Of all of them, Jordan had always been the most generous, the most trusting, and the most easily hurt.

He could understand why Jordan would be drawn to a man like Peter. Alvarez seemed to be in tune with his surroundings, sensitive to the emotions of others. That could be a good thing, or a very bad thing, depending.

"We'll see," Morgan said. Although he directed those words more at himself than at Peter, the other man nodded.

"I hope so," Peter said.

Morgan had the sense Alvarez said *those* words to himself.

"Well, I'd better get back to work. My new boss can be a hard ass when he wants to be," Peter said.

"Yeah, me, too. Considering it's my business we're working on, I guess I should get a move on, as well."

"Maybe we should close this?" Peter said, pointing to the large bay doors.

"I've got it. You go on ahead." Morgan went over to the control panel and closed the automatic doors, then locked them.

He took a moment to look over at the Piper. Maybe it wouldn't hurt to add a little extra security, just in case. Morgan studied the interior of the doors, both the bay doors and the smaller, regular door. They already had an alarm system that would sound not just here, but trigger an alarm at the Sheriff's office and the fire hall. But it wouldn't hurt, for the time being, to put in another, secondary system. One that would notify just him, if the other system was somehow breeched and the hangar entered. He happened to have a few things on hand, and it wouldn't take much jerry-rigging.

The extra layer of security would certainly help him sleep better, too, because he'd decided his gut was telling him that Preston Rogers was trouble, big time.

* * * *

Tamara had been thinking about this for hours. At the damndest times, she'd look over and catch either Morgan or Henry staring at her, and a wave of heat would swamp her. Or she'd catch a private moment between Penelope and her men, see the glow that practically enveloped them, and know exactly what they were thinking, what they were craving.

Those sudden lust attacks had kept her off balance since morning.

"Tamara?"

The question in Morgan's voice stoked her fires. She'd burned all day and needed relief. She didn't doubt the men knew she was wired. She turned to look at them, and the lust that pulsed from them left her in no doubt. They burned, too.

"Yes?" How interesting to play this polite conversational game when what she felt inside her wasn't polite at all.

"Tell us what you need, Red."

Even now, they meant to give her what she needed, what she wanted. Oh, she knew they'd receive their pleasure, so much they'd be exhausted in short order. But they put her first, and had from that first moment.

How could she resist that kind of generosity? She couldn't. She could only sate herself in it and them, and be as generous in return.

"I need you both."

"You can have us both." Henry stepped closer. He reached out and ran his fingers down the side of her face, cupped her cheek, and brought her in for his kiss.

A light brush of his mouth on hers, his heat shimmered right there, for her, and she drank it in, drank him in. Then she leaned away just enough to meet his gaze. She slid a glance at Morgan, who stood ready, she knew, to do whatever it was she asked of him.

"In me at the same time. I want you in me at the same time."

Morgan reached for her and drew her ever so slowly into his arms. "Are you sure?"

Before she could answer him, he laid his lips on hers, a kiss as gentle as his brother's had been. "Be sure, sweetheart. Because this takes us to a whole new level. Can you accept that?"

A part of her wished she could pretend she didn't understand his meaning. But that would be lying—to herself, and to them. At her core, she was an honest woman.

"We're at that level anyway. I thought to keep this just physical. Keep us as friends with benefits. But we're more than that. I don't know if this is forever, what's between us. I know you believe it is, the both of you. I'm not there yet. I don't know if I'll ever be there. Can you accept *that*?"

"Yes." Morgan didn't hesitate. He leaned down, kissed her, then stepped back.

Henry's arm came around her, and he turned her into his kiss. His mouth, hot and wet, caressed and slid, wooing hers, enticing hers to taste and tease until their tongues danced a slow, seductive tango. Henry scooped her into his arms before he broke the kiss.

"I can walk." Although she thought she should be getting used to being carried by these two very macho men.

"Of course you can. This is all part of our 'sweep-her-off-her-feet master plan.'"

Tamara laughed. Henry's wit and dry delivery tickled her sense of humor.

"How's that working for you?" she asked him.

"You're off your feet, and we're about to get lucky," Morgan said. "I'd say it's working pretty well."

They didn't let her catch her breath. Henry lowered her feet to the floor. Then, together, they peeled the clothes from her body.

Hands and mouths stroked and kissed, aroused and seduced. Tamara let them know she wanted equal access and smiled when their impatient movements stripped their own clothes from their bodies.

They brought her to the bed, and she wondered at the frenzy that overtook them all. They touched and tasted, rolled and caressed and cupped and squeezed. She immersed herself in the scent of them, in the feel of their hard muscles and musk-flavored flesh. She wanted, needed, all of them on all of her. As she immersed herself in them, want evolved beyond need, hovering on instinct. *Join, burrow, mesh.* Her psyche pushed her to leave all boundaries behind and tumble, wild and free, into the unknown.

Morgan reached for her, eased her over his body so that she straddled him. The heat of his latex-covered cock against her labia made her pussy clench and release its dew. Then she slid onto him, his erection filling her, the tip of his cock hitting her cervix as she took him all.

He continued to ease her down, until her face rested on his chest while his hands caressed her back.

The sounds of preparation sped the beat of her heart in her chest as excitement spiraled within her. She listened as Henry tore open the condom then rolled it into place. She understood the tiny whir was the sound of the cap being unscrewed from the tube of lube.

He didn't warn her, just used his fingers to smooth a generous amount on her anus, stroking up and down and pushing in a little. Then another wet sound, and she knew he covered his sheathed cock in the gel, too.

All the while, Morgan stroked her back with his hands as his cock gently and slowly stroked the inside of her pussy.

"Easy." The heat of Henry's body close to hers, the movement on the bed behind her, fed her excitement, and yes, her trepidation.

Could her body even hold two cocks this way?

"I'll stop if you ask it." And then she felt the presence of his cock, the hot, round bulb of it, pushing against her anus.

"Oh, God. You feel so hot and big."

"Work yourself back on me, sweetheart. You set the pace."

In tiny increments she pushed against him, the combination of burning and sexual allure a cocktail she immediately loved. Back and forth, she found she could stimulate both cocks, and her hunger for more grew.

"Mm, I need…" She needed more but couldn't talk, as the invasion of two cocks took every ounce of energy, every bit of attention.

"More?"

"Yes."

Henry pressed a little harder. She felt her anus open, and the head of his cock enter her.

"Oh, oh. My…yes…just…" The tingles and shivers of acute horniness seemed to slither and go off everywhere at once. She couldn't focus because it wasn't just one spot that hummed within her, close to climax. Every spot had become an erogenous zone, everywhere quivered with barely held thrills.

"God, sweetheart, you feel so good. I need..." He inched forward just a little. Tamara pushed down and in, and felt Morgan's cock seat itself even deeper inside her pussy.

"I'm going to come," he said.

She felt the beginning spasms of his cock in her cunt as he began to empty himself inside of her. "I...I..." Words deserted her, seemed meaningless when she hovered on the very edge of heaven.

Morgan moved under her, just slightly, and her clit brushed the hair at the base of his cock.

"Oh!" The orgasm came like a tidal wave, full and deep and wonderful, so wonderful she began to bounce, tiny movements that made Henry swear and begin to thrust inside her.

"Yes, oh, *Tamara*." Henry's cock slid deep, and he began to pump in her, a mindless, completely feral action and reaction that felt wild and wonderful. Friction ignited within her, burning her with a climax that kept flooding her with surge after surge of total and complete bliss.

She welcomed his weight on her, the feel and the sound of his struggle for breath and the sound of Morgan's heart pounding under her ear.

"God in Heaven." Henry's low rumble could have been a prayer.

Tamara began to shake as tiny aftershocks of ecstasy shivered through her and made her teeth chatter.

"Are you all right?" Henry's question echoed through her.

She smiled, and her smile felt as sexy as hell. "I'm way beyond all right, flyboy. I think we hit the stratosphere."

"We aim to please." Henry huffed those words against her neck.

Tamara giggled, even as she realized these two lovers of hers had told the absolute truth earlier. She didn't think there'd be any going back, either.

Chapter 17

The Lusty Community Center had been built just last year—another Kendall Construction project, Tamara learned, to replace the aging and far too small recreation hall which the town had erected in the 1930s.

For this occasion, the interior of what they referred to as the great room sported festive decorations in white, teal blue and deep magenta. The space brimmed with people. The mix of voices created a platform of sound from which music softly rose. Country melodies of guitars and a drum and a fiddle filled the air. No DJ spun records or played CDs for this party. The entertainment came courtesy of a four-person combo in the back corner of the room.

Tables had been set up to one side, and one of the longest buffets Tamara had ever seen lined the far wall. All around her, people were smiling and hugging, laughing and chatting. The party mood seemed very much alive and well this late Saturday afternoon.

Samantha had already filled in some of the less personal details of today's event. Rather than a formal affair, with seats assigned and the pomp of ushers, bridesmaids, and best men, a Lusty Commitment Ceremony was casual and friendly. Guests stood while vows were given and received, and then the celebrating began right afterward.

As much as Tamara was grateful to the woman for that information, what she really wanted to know about was the nuts and bolts of the arrangement itself. How on earth did all of these families manage to make it work? Her own parents hadn't been able to hold it together, and there'd been only two of them. In the end, she reasoned who better to ask a personal question of than the men with whom she currently enjoyed a personal relationship?

"So tell me, how does this work, exactly? I've never been to a wedding featuring one bride and two grooms."

Morgan chuckled. "Sometimes I forget the entire world doesn't live this way." He had a good hold of one of her hands, and Henry had the other. They led her to the right, looking for a bit of open floor where they could see the white wooden trellis that had been set up—presumably where the ceremony itself would take place.

"It's really very simple," Morgan said. "The oldest male becomes the legal husband—we can't, after all, circumvent the laws of the land. That's why this is called a commitment ceremony, rather than a marriage ceremony. Here, the three of them will pledge themselves to *each other*, creating a new family. All members of that new family vow to love and support one another."

"The oldest is the legal husband? What about in the case of twins—or triplets?" She thought of Morgan and Henry's own fathers, who were triplets.

"One of the reasons keeping track of the birth time is kind of crucial," Henry said. "Our father, Preston, was the first born, arriving two and four minutes before his brothers Taylor and Charles, respectively."

"The legal marriage is the formality," Morgan said. "And by the time Susan and those Wildcatters get here today, it would already have taken place. This is the important part, right here. These are the vows that matter the most."

"Why is that?" Tamara found she didn't mind having both her hands held hostage. She also discovered she couldn't resist smiling back at so many happy, smiling faces.

"Our kind of family—a ménage family—is more complicated, structurally. The husbands have a special obligation to make certain that jealousy never festers between them and that their wife never feels her loyalties are being divided. They have to work together to be a solid unit upon which the wife, and later the children, can depend."

"Sounds like a good deal for the wife and kids." She couldn't help but let thoughts from her own familial experience seep in. Neither of her parents had ever proven to be anything other than selfish, immature people. "But what about the husbands? What's in it for them?"

"Sweetheart, the husbands are the real winners," Henry said. "They get a perpetually happy and satisfied wife. Women have always held the real power in relationships, you know. Forget about gender and pay equality. At the very base of our society, the truth is that if a wife is unhappy, her entire family is unhappy, too."

"There are always tough times in life." Morgan's expression turned serious. "I've seen it happen at nearly every base I've been stationed. Sometimes the burden of worry can break a man, or destroy a marriage, or both." He took a moment to bring her hand up to his mouth for a kiss. "One of the things our dads always say is that they really don't know what that kind of heartbreak or despair feels like, because they've always had each other to turn to, so none of them has ever felt as if it's just himself alone fighting the dragons of the world."

That was an aspect of family Tamara had never experienced, the sense of being a part of a unit, of caring for each other and working together.

Goodwin's laugh boomed out and her eyes sought him in the crowd. *No, that last thought isn't true at all.*

Her gaze found him standing not that far away, talking to Kate Benedict and three other men, one of whom was on crutches.

She may not know what it's like to be loved and cherished by her birth parents, but from the time she'd dumped herself on his doorstep, her great-uncle Goodwin had been as good a father to her as any man could be.

In a heartbeat she recalled all the important moments. How he'd settled them in a house with land so she could have a garden and a dog. How he'd sat with her while she struggled with her high school algebra, and how he'd taken her part against the principal after she'd defended herself against bullies.

He'd mourned with her when that dog, Viceroy, had died of old age, even making a grave marker for him in the backyard beneath the tree he'd so loved to sleep under.

Uncle Goodwin had given her flying lessons, and discipline, and space, and he'd been there for her every single day since she was sixteen years old.

Tamara blinked. This was a strange time and place for an epiphany, but she supposed they came when they would. "Excuse me for a minute." She extricated her hands from her lovers and wove her way through the crowd until she stood beside her uncle.

Without warning him, she stretched up and placed a kiss on his cheek.

"Well now, that was very nice. Did I do anything to deserve it?" He beamed down at her, and his smile made hers bloom wider.

"As a matter of fact, yes, you did. You've been a good father to me. I just wanted you to know I appreciate it."

Goodwin blushed, but pleasure shone in his eyes. "Hell, girl, you made that easy enough. Truth is, I'm grateful you came and put some excitement into this old bachelor's life. So right back at you, Tamara Jones. You've been a good daughter to me."

"Even though I couldn't get that Piper home last Tuesday?"

Goodwin laughed. "Even though. But I have a feeling your having landed here, when you did, was meant to be."

A hand on her shoulder told her the flyboys had followed her. Morgan gave her a gentle squeeze and took her right hand back at the same time Henry clasped her left again.

"I was just introducing Goodwin to the fathers of the bride and grooms," Kate said. "Tamara, this is Caleb and Jonathan Benedict. And this Mike Murphy—he's the father of Colt and Ryder."

Tamara congratulated the men on the occasion. The three of them looked pleased as punch their kids were making a new family. They excused themselves to go stand up near the arbor, as the guests of honor would be arriving soon.

Kate followed after them, after she'd bestowed hugs and kisses on Morgan and Henry. It startled Tamara to be included in that tradition. The show of affection had been a grandmotherly gesture and another new experience for her.

"There you are. I thought we could all sit together later." Jordan looked as if he'd just arrived after having gotten ready in a rush. Trailing him were Jake, and Peter Alvarez.

"Sounds like a plan," Morgan agreed. "Where's Adam? He get stuck staying on duty?"

"No, Jasper's manning the Sheriff's office today. Adam is looking for Ginny. He's going to try and persuade her to join us," Jake said.

He's excited by the prospect. Tamara thought of the shy waitress and wondered how she'd feel about being courted by these two Kendalls. Adam seemed a calm and steady force, but Jake struck her as being a little more aggressive and adventurous. Jake's gaze seemed to come to rest over her shoulder, and she could tell, just by the expression on his face, that his brother had been successful.

"Snagged us a couple of pretty girls to brighten up our table," Adam said. He winked at Tamara. "Not that you're not pretty, Ms. Jones."

"You don't mind if I join you?" Tracy Jessop stood close to Ginny, and Tamara might have thought she'd only come over for Ginny's benefit, if the young sous-chef hadn't directed her question at Jordan.

Jordan returned her smile then introduced her to Peter.

Tamara had the sense that there were definite sparks between Tracy and Jordan—unless she was mistaking familial bonds for something more. Then she thought Peter's eyes showed more than a spark of appreciation when he looked at the young woman, too. *Isn't that interesting?*

"We don't mind one bit, honey. Why don't we try to edge our way a little closer to the front?" Jordan maneuvered himself so that Tracy ended up between him and Peter, putting Jake closer to Ginny.

"Good idea," Morgan said. Since he still had Tamara's hand, she followed when he led her back toward their previous spot.

Applause erupted and with the rest of the assembly, Tamara turned her attention to the front of the hall, and the celebrants who'd just entered.

* * * *

It was the hardest thing Preston had ever done, driving away from that Piper the day before. Every instinct in him screamed at him to move on it, then and there. Of course he knew he couldn't. He needed to get his bearings, get his men in place, and learn what he could of the airfield and the people who ran it, as soon as possible.

Only fools rushed in, and ended up behind bars for their trouble. Or in his case, first behind bars and *then* dead. Miguel Ramos had a very long reach.

They'd taken rooms out by the Interstate, because the town of Lusty, Texas apparently had no visitor accommodations.

He'd dined late Friday afternoon at a restaurant called Lusty Appetites, and while there hit upon his first piece of good luck since this entire misbegotten adventure had begun.

He'd been getting ready to leave when he overheard a conversation between one of the waitresses and a customer.

"Hey, Ginny, what time is Kelsey staying open till tomorrow?"

"Hey, Mr. Parker. Kelsey's planning to close around noon, sharp," the waitress said. "That ought to give us enough time to get set up over at the community center for the shindig there at four."

"That's fine, then. I'll bring myself here for breakfast and then get dinner over at the ceremony. Don't 'spect she'll be posting a sign about the closure, will she?"

"She said she was going to, even though most folks in Lusty will be attending the ceremony anyway and will figure she's closed."

"Well, she's still new to town, even if she is a Benedict now." Then the customer snorted. "But then, I asked, didn't I?"

"Yes, sir, you sure did. Can I get you some dessert, Mr. Parker?"

"Now, Ginny Rose, when you going to get around to calling me Albert?"

"Oh, I can't do that, Mr. Parker. I was raised to show respect to my betters."

Preston wondered what kind of tip the old geezer was going to give Ginny Rose. Hell, if it weren't for the fact that it would draw attention to himself, he'd leave her a big one himself.

Instead, Preston had paid his bill, left a moderate tip, then gotten in his car and headed back to the motel.

Now, nearly twenty-four hours later, they were going over all their intel and putting the final touches on their plan.

"It's like the entire freaking town is shutting down for whatever the hell it is going on today at the community center," Dennis said.

"It's a wedding, from what I gathered," Jimmy said. "One of the clerks at the grocery thought I was a friend of the groom who apparently isn't from around here." He tilted his head to one side. "It would seem they do things differently here in Lusty."

Preston waved his hand in a dismissive gesture. He wasn't particularly interested in how they did things in Lusty. His only concern was working out the best plan for getting into that hangar and getting his hands on Ramos' property without getting caught.

"So it's just an afternoon affair?"

"No, from what I gather it's going to last most of the night and on into the morning," Dennis said. "It was the person at the hardware store I spoke to, and he assumed I was a friend of the groom, too."

"Yeah, that's the impression I got, that the party would run late," Jimmy said. "As to the rest of the town, there's a sheriff's office, fire hall, clinic. That's the sum total of the high-tech institutions Lusty can claim. Not a very big place, from what I could see."

Two sharp knocks sounded on the door followed by two more. Preston nodded, and Dennis opened it and let Lorne in.

"Well?"

"I found a way onto the airfield that doesn't have us using the gates. That's the good news. The bad news is we'll have to hoof it a good mile from there. Here." He came over to the table and looked down at the map. "There's this road, here, and right about there," he pinpointed a spot, "we can park and walk through that copse of trees, and we're on the field."

"Good. They'll have the hangars wired for security—likely the gate, too, which is why I'm glad we won't have to use it."

"It's such a Podunk town, maybe they won't have it wired," Dennis said.

"There's a brand new-looking Learjet in that hangar next to the Piper. Bet your ass it'll be wired, and wired well. Jimmy?"

"I'll do a search online and see if I can come up with any specs on their security setup. We've got a few hours, so I can hit a couple security companies, hack into their systems. Otherwise, I think I can get us in if we take our time. Easiest way would be to put a stint into the power lines leading to the installation, but that would leave us in the dark inside. I'll know best what to do in an hour or so."

"I don't want to risk any more encroachments, either at the airfield or in the town." Preston got up, poured himself some coffee from the small in-room pot. "The fact that you two were asked if you were there for the wedding tells me they take note of strangers. So we'll let Jimmy do his computer magic while the three of us head into

Waco to get the equipment we'll need for tonight. We can't assume there's no on-site live security, so we go in hot. And we do that a couple hours after dark."

"Wait for the party to get into full swing and the partygoers to be on their way to getting drunk," Jimmy said.

"Yeah." Preston met his second's gaze. "And when we do go in, I want just Jimmy and me on the inside." Jimmy was the only one besides him who knew exactly what they were looking for, and where to find it. Preston trusted his other two men, to a certain extent. But then, he'd trusted the Piper's pilot, too. "Dennis, you and Lorne will be outside and perimeter security. Maybe this will come off without a hitch. But I'm not making any more assumptions."

"How do you want us to handle any nosy Nancy's who poke their noses in?" Dennis asked.

"Quietly, and if possible, without killing anyone. I mean it, Dennis. I don't want any more accidents like the one you had with Frank West. We're businessmen, not murderers."

Dennis looked uncomfortable with the reminder that he'd fucked up. *Good.* If at any time things went south, they didn't want the specter of a death sentence staring them in the face.

He turned to Jimmy. "You get busy. The rest of us will head into Waco." He took a moment to meet the gaze of each of his men. "We can't fail, tonight. If we do, our lives aren't going to be worth shit."

Chapter 18

"He's just making points all over the damn place tonight, isn't he?"

Tamara smiled. Morgan's words, for her ears alone, somehow tickled her.

The flyboys had each proven themselves to be masters on the dance floor. At the moment the band was playing something slow, which allowed her the opportunity to press herself against Morgan's firm and deliciously hard body. The evening was still young, and she'd enjoyed a couple more drinks than usual for her. Far from being drunk she instead felt very relaxed and mellow. She'd spent the evening dancing with her two handsome dates, and getting to know their brothers and some of their many, many cousins.

She brought her attention back to her current dance partner. Morgan looked so cute when he grumbled. She didn't have to ask him who he was grumbling about, either. Instead, she asked, "What's Mr. Alvarez doing *now* that's got your goat?"

"He's dancing with Kate Benedict."

Tamara's smile widened. Morgan had been just as vexed a half hour earlier when Peter had been dancing with his mother, Samantha.

Of course, she'd noticed Adam following the man with a narrowed gaze, too—when he wasn't trying to coax Ginny Rose out onto the dance floor.

"What is it about Peter that you and Adam don't like, exactly?"

"I never said I didn't like him. I do agree with Adam's assessment, though. It just seems there's more to the man than meets the eye. And you do have to admit he's moved pretty fast to ingratiate himself with the families, considering we've all just met him this week. Dancing with Mom, then Kate. It's like he's figured out who the most powerful members of the family are and is trying to worm his way into their good graces. It's working, too, damn it."

Tamara eased back just a little so she could meet Morgan's gaze. "Or maybe he's just trying to be sociable…and you didn't just say that, about his moving fast on such short acquaintance. You, of all people."

Morgan tilted his head to one side. She saw the exact moment he understood her point. He chuckled and shook his head, then drew her back into his arms, against his chest.

"That was a little hypocritical of me, wasn't it?"

"Maybe just a little," she said.

"So bite me. I'm the protective sort." The words puffed against her hair just before he kissed the top of her head.

"I never would have guessed that about you." Tamara closed her eyes, trusting Morgan to guide her around the dance floor. Considering that she'd been reluctant at first to attend a family event, it had proven to be wonderful party, the best she'd ever attended. The entire day had been special.

Tamara had never thought of herself as the emotional type, but when first Susan, and then Colt and Ryder, had recited the vows they'd each written, she'd been unashamed of the tears in her eyes.

Most men are fortunate if they have one miracle in their lives. I've been gifted with two, and I'll gladly spend the rest of my life living my gratitude for you, Colt, and you, Susan.

"I wonder what their story is," she mused, thinking of the words Ryder had spoken earlier.

"Whose story?"

"Colt and Ryder's. I felt such emotion coming from them both, earlier. I think I can almost understand how brothers could trust each other and care for each other enough to share a wife. But friends?" She'd spent a lot of time this day thinking about the kinds of families that seemed to abound in Lusty, Texas. Everyone appeared so damn happy, and that happiness wasn't the thin veneer put on for social situations. It was real and genuine and deep.

Standing back and looking at these people, then looking at her own family, she could only come to the conclusion that in order to make such an arrangement work, the people here must be truly extraordinary.

"Sweetheart, not all brothers are born. Some are chosen. My understanding is that Colt and Ryder have been best friends since childhood—that both were street kids who relied upon each other for survival."

Tamara thought about that for a moment. "I guess as bad as my childhood was, it could have been a lot worse."

"Yes," Morgan said. "And just because a past has been fractured doesn't mean the future can't be wonderful."

Tamara followed Morgan's gaze. Adam had succeeded in his quest to get Ginny to dance, even if she was doing so a little stiffly.

Were Morgan's words meant for the waitress, or for herself?

When the musicians announced a small break, Tamara and Morgan joined the large table appropriated by the Kendalls. Although most people circulated during the band breaks, so having a seat saved didn't necessarily mean you had a seat saved. When Henry snagged her around the waist, she laughed as he set her on his lap, claiming a shortage of chairs. Morgan took the chair to the right of them.

Adam brought Ginny over to the table.

"Now, Adam, I don't think your family wants me sitting here the entire—"

"Sure they do, Ginny." Adam guided her toward an empty chair.

"Welcome back, Ginny. Please sit with us for a while longer. All of us rough-and-tumble men need more pretty girls to smooth out our rough edges." Henry's smile seemed to disarm the other woman as well as it did Tamara.

Ginny shook her head. "Don't think there's sandpaper enough in all of Texas for that job," she said.

"You sit, and I'll get *you* a drink for a change," Adam said.

"I really should see if Kelsey needs any—"

"Kelsey told you to relax and have fun, don't you remember?" Adam said.

"Boy howdy, Adam Kendall! Do you *never* let a woman finish a sentence?"

"Not if that sentence is going to be an excuse to retreat. Sit with us a while, Ginny. Please? Enjoy the party with us. You know everyone here."

Tamara held her breath—with the rest of the table—as she waited to see what Ginny would say. She looked down for a moment, and there was enough light for Tamara to see her face wore a blush of embarrassment. Then she sighed.

"All right. Thank you."

"No, thank you. Now what would you like to drink?"

"Just a cola, please, Adam."

"That's all I'm drinking tonight, too, so two colas coming right up."

Ginny's gaze followed him as he made his way over to where the bar had been set up. She shook her head. "Bossy as the day is long," she said softly.

When she realized there were so many of his brothers close by, she got a stricken look on her face.

"They're all bossy," Tamara said. She waved her hand to include Jake, Jordan, and Peter, who were sitting on the other side of the table. "It's in the genes I think. The secret to keeping your sanity is to understand they can't help themselves. You have to just let them be bossy, and then carry on and do what you were going to do, anyway."

"That's the pure truth, Ginny," Tracy said. "I've lived here all my life, and I can tell you there's not a Kendall, Benedict, or Jessop male ever born didn't excel at being bossy." Then she grinned. "But you will note it's the women—Kate, Bernice, Samantha and Anna—that hold the real power here. They make the men tremble in their boots."

Tamara smiled at Ginny, pleased when the woman laughed.

Feeling a stare she looked up and encountered Jake's mockingly fierce gaze. "You've been speaking to Mom, haven't you?" he asked.

"Oh, you bet I have. At every opportunity."

"Mom loaned Tamara her brand-new Caddy to drive. What does that tell you?" Henry asked his younger brother.

Jake smirked. "It tells me you and Morgan are toast." He raised his beer bottle in salute.

Adam came back with two glasses of cola. He set one in front of Ginny and took the seat next to her. "Ginny, Mom said to tell you hi and hopes you're still on for lunch tomorrow," he said.

Morgan and Henry, along with Jordan and Peter, snickered. Ginny just grinned and ducked her head to try and hide it.

"Okay, what did I miss?" Adam asked.

Morgan took a sip from his bottle of beer then set it down. "Not telling, little brother. It's one of those things in life that is better if you find out on your own. I'll be back in a few," he said.

Tamara watched him walk away, figuring he was making a trip to the bathroom. Instead, he headed toward the front of the center, and the door to the outside.

She turned to ask Henry where his brother was headed, but the band had returned and began to play.

"My turn to dance with a pretty woman," Henry said.

It was really ridiculous, the ease with which he lifted her off his lap. "Hang on a moment."

"I plan to hang on a lot longer than just a moment, don't you worry there, Itty. I have no intention of dropping you." Henry made that outrageous statement as he carried her to the dance floor.

"I wanted to ask you where Morgan went," she said as Henry drew her close and began to dance with her.

"I know you did, sweetheart. I just preferred you do so here, where the others can't hear us. He's gone to check on something out at the airfield."

"Now? It's pitch dark out, and there's a party going on. What does he need to check on now?"

"He set an electronic alarm on the door to one of the hangars. If triggered, it would send an alert to his cell phone."

"And he's going out there *alone* to check on it?"

"Well, I did think I would follow him in a few minutes. Not that I doubt Morgan can handle himself—he has had occasion to so in the past, on a regular basis. But he is my favorite brother, and I'd feel better having his back."

"Tell me again there're no black ops in the Air Force."

Henry chuckled. "So after this dance I'll return you to the table and head to the airfield to back him up. All right?"

"No. After this dance we'll both head out to the airfield."

"Tamara—"

"Don't you 'Tamara' me, Henry Kendall. I brought that plane here. If there's trouble because of it, then by damn I'll help deal with it."

"And you call *us* bossy."

For once she didn't let his grin affect her. She just kept giving him a level stare until he sighed. "You can come along. But damn it, woman, if I say duck, you duck."

Tamara nodded, not because she agreed, of course, but because she understood. The flyboys felt bound and determined to act macho and keep the little lady safe.

Only trouble with that mindset was the little lady in question felt just as determined to protect them, too.

* * * *

Morgan didn't see any vehicles in the compound when he drove past the airfield. The front gate appeared closed and locked, just as he'd left it earlier that day. Everything looked good and secure.

His instincts screamed otherwise. Something had set off the alarm he'd rigged just inside the hangar door, and he doubted it would have been anything as innocuous as a mouse or a stray cat.

He drove past the gates for another quarter mile before he pulled the car to the side of the road and turned it off.

He eased out of the vehicle, and only stopped long enough to pull a few necessary items out of the trunk of his car.

One was his Glock 9 mm handgun.

He changed out of his dress boots, slipping into his athletic shoes. Exchanging sport coat for sweater, he lowered the trunk silently then felt in his pocket for the small penlight he always carried. Clouds obscured the moon, which he counted as a positive. He'd use the light if he had to, but he doubted he would.

It didn't take long to run the short distance back toward the airfield. He had the key for the gate but instead veered off into the bushes so he could climb the fence that ran most of the perimeter of the installation.

A good hundred yards spread out between his position and the hangars. Keeping himself low to the ground, Morgan sprinted the distance. Coming up against the building he flattened himself against the wall and listened. No sounds disturbed the stillness of the night. Rather than work his way around to the front, he chose to keep to the back, keeping his senses on alert for danger. As he inched his way along the wall, a flash of light snagged his attention. Ahead of him, at the end of the building, someone lit a cigarette.

He held still, clinging to the shadows, and watched as that person took a few drags and seemed to be watching toward the north and the trees that stretched out from there to the road. Then the man turned and disappeared behind the end of the building.

Morgan moved quickly and had the back door to the helicopter hangar open in seconds. He slipped inside.

This space felt empty, and of course it would be. Whoever was here had broken in next door.

Along the wall separating the two hangars, a service door had been installed but seldom used. Morgan had taken the time just after planting his alarm to ensure the thing stood unblocked, unlocked, and didn't squeak when opened.

Morgan eased it open now and moved silently into the next hangar.

"One car drove past, but kept going. You want me to jimmy the lock on the Piper, boss?"

"No, Dennis, I'll get it. I need you to keep your eyes peeled outside."

The man called Dennis nodded and headed back outside, closing the door behind him. The man who'd presented himself the day before looking to hire a flight to New York stood staring at the plane. He stepped forward, tested the door handle.

It was locked, of course.

He reached inside his pocket, pulled something out, and bent to the task.

Morgan, gun in hand, moved quickly and stealthily until he stood behind Preston Rogers.

"You're trespassing. Again. I'm going to have to ask you to raise your hands and turn around, slowly."

Preston Rogers straightened and turned to face Morgan.

"Looks like you caught me red-handed. Just curious. How did you know I was here?"

"You tripped an alarm." Morgan's gut clenched. Something wasn't right. Rogers should be sweating, not smiling.

"That's funny. Jimmy says he disabled the alarm. Didn't you, Jimmy?"

"I thought I did."

Morgan froze. That voice had come from behind him. Then the press of cold metal against the back of his neck brought all his instincts to a grinding halt.

"I'll take this." Rogers relieved him of his Glock.

The man flicked the safety on then tucked the gun into his waistband. "When I'm done here, we'll get Dennis in to take care of this complication."

"I didn't come alone." Morgan was feeling like a raw recruit. He'd not given this Rogers character enough credit for smarts. All he could do now was try and bluff his way into a position of being able to overpower his captors as soon as the opportunity arose.

Sure. Easy job. Nothing to it.

"Yes, you did come alone. If you really had a partner with you, you'd never give it—or I should say him—away. You jokers who wear the white hats are just too damn noble for your own good and always play by the same, outdated rules."

"Maybe my hat isn't as white as you think. Or maybe, I'm just following another script."

Preston Rogers chuckled. He checked his watch. "Not even ten, yet. I imagine that party you came from is going strong. Won't be anyone looking for you till morning, most likely."

Rogers turned back to the Piper. He bent to look at the door lock.

"Don't suppose you have the key?" he asked Morgan.

"Sorry. I wasn't planning on going for a flight tonight. Especially not in a plane with a bum engine."

Rogers grinned. "So that's why it's here. I wondered. Don't worry. I didn't plan on flying it, either. Now that other one, over there, she looks like she'd be one sweet ride."

Morgan wondered if he could make Jimmy relax enough he could nail him and use him as a shield against Rogers. *It could probably work*. By the time Rogers pulled his gun, he'd have Jimmy by the throat and in front of him.

But then, if there truly was no honor among criminals, Rogers would just shoot Jimmy and then shoot him, too.

And he couldn't forget the third man in this little gang, the one Rogers had called Dennis.

"Too bad you'll never know—about the Learjet, that is."

Rogers shrugged. "Doesn't matter." Then he gave Morgan a considering look. "I only came for what's my property. Once I have it, you can keep the Piper. I just want what's in her."

"What's in her?"

"Watch, and be amazed. Or better yet, don't watch. Jimmy, take our guest to the lounge, and don't give him a chance to deck you."

Jimmy laughed from behind him and took a step back, effectively eliminating Morgan's chance to do just that, deck him. "Don't worry, boss. I've got this one under control. Move it, white hat."

"Why don't we all just stay where we are?" Henry's voice, clear and cold, came from behind them all. "With one exception, of course. Jimmy, be a nice boy and let my brother have your gun."

Chapter 19

Tamara didn't like having to hide in the bushes like a scared little rabbit. She kept her eyes focused on where Henry had just slunk out of sight, along the back of the hangar. It felt as if minutes stretched to hours since he'd been gone. They knew Morgan was in trouble, because he hadn't answered his cell phone when Henry had called.

Now Tamara couldn't escape the dreadful feeling that Henry was going to be walking in trouble, too.

What should she do?

She'd never been in a situation like this before, but that didn't stop her from thinking, and it sure didn't stop her instincts from screaming at her to do *something*. She was far from dumb, not at all clumsy, and had more than a move or two up her sleeve.

Unfortunately, she had a feeling that whoever it was her lovers faced likely ranked a few notches higher on the danger scale than the high school bullies she'd bested.

Regardless, the realization that one or both of the men she loved could be in serious peril meant she couldn't just stand by, hiding, and do nothing at all.

Oh, crap. There it was, the thought she'd been avoiding like the plague. A part of her had figured that as long as she didn't think the words, she could continue to fool herself that what she felt for those damn flyboys was nothing more than affectionate lust.

Maybe I am a dumb broad. A smart woman would have kept her emotions at the "affectionate lust" level.

She wouldn't have gone and fallen all the way in love with them both.

Tamara ran a shaking hand through her hair. This was no time to be thinking hearts and flowers, for God's sake.

"Okay, first thing, get closer. And second thing, stop talking to yourself." Tamara recalled how Henry had moved, low and fast, toward the corner of the hangar. About two hundred feet of open ground separated her from the building. She could do this. But not without making a bit of a sacrifice, first.

She looked down at the stylish pumps she'd bought the day before and without remorse kicked them off. She was dressed for a party, not skullduggery. She couldn't run in pumps.

Her gaze wandered over to the construction site. Would there be something there she could use as a weapon? Henry had carried a handgun, an item she'd had no idea he possessed until he'd grabbed it out of the trunk of the car. She didn't have a gun, but she would feel better if she had some sort of weapon on hand.

Tamara ran across the grass, biting down on the urge to swear when grass turned to dirt and bits of gravel dug into her stocking-covered feet. Moving through the place where just the day before she'd been working and bantering, she searched for something she could use as a means of defense.

The crowbar that had been left leaning against one wall would be perfect, but when she picked it up, it proved to be way too heavy. Finally, she found a screwdriver, one that was not much more than a couple of inches long. The good news was she could easily conceal it in her hand. The bad news, of course, was that it wouldn't be good for much except up close. Very close.

She would have liked something more substantial, but she wasn't certain how much time had passed while she'd been searching. She needed to get into that hangar, and she needed do it *now*.

Clouds continued to obscure the moon and stars, and no outdoor lights illuminated the path from where she hid to where she needed to be. She wasn't certain if the back door to the helicopter hangar was open or not, and if it was, how could she get into the other part where she knew in her gut everyone was? She wished she'd asked Henry what he'd planned to do, exactly.

Maybe she could sneak around to the front and go right in the main door. If her men were in danger, if they were involved in some kind of a face-off against—well, against whomever—perhaps she could sneak in, unnoticed. Maybe they'd be too busy to see her.

That sure as hell wasn't much of a plan, but it was all she could come up with.

Tamara scanned the entire area. She saw no one and nothing moving, so she crouched as low as she could and ran across the open ground, not daring to breathe until she reached the cold solid outside wall of the hangar. She waited, listening, but heard nothing. The corner of the building lay just ahead. Once she rounded it, she'd be on the north side, a short side of the building. The door was just around the next corner after that, along the long, west-facing outside wall. She could do this. She *would* do this.

Inhaling deeply, clutching the screwdriver close, she mentally prepared to run.

Grabbed from behind, she had no time to scream as a hand fastened over her mouth and another clamped against her waist.

"Do not move, or make a sound, or you'll be very, *very* sorry. Do you understand me?"

Tamara couldn't see who had her, but then, she didn't need to. Her heart sank as she recognized the voice of Peter Alvarez.

* * * *

Henry had assessed the situation and known he only had one chance to get it right.

Thank God, he had.

"Son of a bitch. You weren't bluffing," the man Jimmy had called boss said to Morgan.

Morgan had already spun around and grabbed Jimmy's gun. Henry felt his tension ease considerably now that the tables had been turned.

"You okay?" he asked his brother.

"A little embarrassed for not having seen this second bruiser," Morgan replied, using his thumb to indicate Jimmy. "But otherwise, yeah, I'm fine. Took you long enough."

"Sorry, I had an itty-bitty complication. Do you want to call Adam, or shall I?"

"In a minute." Morgan walked over to the man standing, hands raised, close enough to the Piper he could lean against it. "You want to tell me what this is all about, Rogers?"

"Listen, white hat, you have no idea what the hell it is you've stepped into. Just let me get what I need to get, and get gone. It's nothing to you, or anyone else here, for that matter. But I warn you. Stop me, and you'll be inviting a world of pain and misery down on this sleepy little burg of yours."

Henry didn't like the sound of that at all. He shot a gaze at Morgan, who only shrugged. "I have no idea," Morgan said. "But there is one more member of this gang, so if you'll keep an eye on the door—"

That door opened and Henry felt his heart leap to his throat.

"Let me go, you son of a bitch!"

Another man entered, gun drawn, his beefy hand wrapped tightly around Tamara's right arm as he dragged her into the hangar.

"Get your hands off of her!" Morgan stepped forward, gun pointed at the new arrival.

The man shrugged and raised his gun to point it directly at Tamara's head.

"Ah, Dennis, what excellent timing," Rogers said. "Gentlemen, your guns, please."

Henry met Morgan's gaze and read the truth in his eyes. Though both wanted to murder the man who'd dared put his hands on their woman, they really had no choice but to surrender their weapons.

"Damn it, Itty. I told you to stay put. Are you all right?"

"Yeah, the gorilla here has a grip just like a gorilla, but I'm ok." Then she narrowed her gaze at Rogers. "Hey, asshole, get away from my Piper."

"*Your* Piper?" He shook his head. "Actually, this plane last belonged to a man in my employ, a greedy little pilot by the name of Frank West." He ran a hand through his hair. "This party's getting way too crowded for my tastes. It's time I just get what I came for and get the hell out of here."

He turned and reached for the door to the plane.

"Looking for these, Rogers?"

Henry's gaze shot to the left, toward a voice that had come from out of the shadows. A couple of footsteps preceded the appearance of Peter Alvarez, a gun held in his right hand, a cloth pouch dangling from his left.

"Who the hell are you?" Rogers demanded.

"It would seem I'm the cavalry." He used his gun as a pointer. "You'll want to tell your goon to take his hands off the lady. Otherwise, I do believe the Kendalls, here, will beat him to bloody death."

Henry shifted just subtly, decreasing the distance slightly between himself and Jimmy, who'd moved so he could cover him and his brother at the same time.

"Or I could tell Dennis to just kill her," Rogers said.

Peter nodded. "Yes, you could. But then, I'd have to kill Dennis, and while ol' Jimmy, here, could maybe get one of the Kendalls, he wouldn't be able to get both, so then he'd die, too. Of course by then I'd have also killed you. That's a whole lot of unnecessary killing, don't you think?"

Henry noticed Morgan shift just a little, too. Jimmy's attention seemed to be going between Peter and his boss.

Just a few more inches, Henry knew, and they'd be able to move. Morgan could take Jimmy. Henry would launch himself toward their woman.

"You're bluffing." Rogers sounded convinced, but Henry noticed the slight doubt in his eyes.

"No, actually, I'm not. I'm offering a fair trade—these very valuable, uncut diamonds, which, by the way, I removed from behind the pilot's seat in the Piper while it was still in John Smith's barn, which also would have been the same time I put the GPS device in it so I could track it—for everyone walking away from here, safe and sound."

Rogers narrowed his eyes. "Who the hell *are* you?"

"Oh, sorry, I didn't introduce myself, did I? What would my mother think of my bad manners? I'm Special Agent Peter Alvarez, Justice Department, Drug Enforcement Agency."

"And you expect me to believe you're just going to let me walk with a fistful of uncut diamonds? You, a fed? What will you tell your bosses?" Rogers scoffed.

Henry shifted. He hoped to hell Peter had a plan because he didn't think Rogers was going to be reasonable. Then he noticed that Peter had edged his way closer to Tamara. Their woman, for her part, seemed to be standing unnaturally still and quiet.

"Shit happens," Peter said.

Everything seemed to happen at once. Tamara raised her left hand and brought it back, hard and fast, ramming Dennis' leg. The man screamed and dropped his gun.

Morgan moved toward Jimmy and Henry dove for Tamara. He wrapped his arms around her and pulled her to the floor, rolling to protect her.

Two gunshots rang out, and the door to the outside burst open. "Freeze! Hands where I can see them!"

Henry sighed as the voice of his brother, Adam, took command of the situation. The sound of several pairs of feet running inside the hangar let Henry know the real cavalry had arrived.

"You flyboys seem to enjoy tackling me," Tamara grumbled from beneath him.

Henry smiled. "I love you, too, sweetheart."

"Shit, you went and got your damn stupid ass shot when you promised you wouldn't!"

The words galvanized Henry, and Tamara too, apparently, because she scrambled to her feet and turned with him to face the others.

Rogers was on the floor, with Adam kneeling on his back as he slapped handcuffs on him. Jimmy lay still, bleeding on the concrete, while Matthew Benedict stood in a two-handed police stance, his gun trained on Dennis, who held his leg and whimpered like a baby.

Henry's gaze sought Morgan, and he sighed with relief when he saw him, whole and uninjured, heading toward their brother Jordan, currently producing a very creative string of cuss words.

Henry, with Tamara in tow, followed.

"Yeah, yeah," Peter said. Sitting on the floor, his right hand clutched his left arm. From between his fingers, blood glistened. "A little dustup now and then goes with the territory. You better accept that right from the get-go. Now, do you want to quit your swearing and give me a hand, here?"

"Tell me, do your family parties always get this exciting?" Tamara asked no one in particular.

Henry laughed. "Only if we're lucky."

* * * *

They'd missed the traditional send-off of the newlyweds. Tamara thought, all things considered, that was probably just as well. It meant the newlyweds had also missed having the "dustup at the airfield," as Peter had called it, infringe on their special day.

Jordan and Matthew had taken Peter to the clinic, where the doctor on duty had seen to his wound. Thankfully, the bullet just grazed him. Dr. James Jessop had disinfected and stitched and made Peter promise he'd keep the sling on for at least the next couple of days.

Then they'd brought him back to the community center. Jordan stood next to Peter, his arms crossed over his chest, the look on his face a mixture of anger and worry.

"I think you bribed your uncle the doctor to give me that shot in the ass *just* so you could get a cheap thrill," Peter accused him.

"It pays to have family," Jordan said. "That's all I'm saying on the subject. It pays to have family."

Peter looked at the assembled group of Benedicts, Kendalls, and Jessops, several of whom had joined the impromptu posse he'd organized at the last minute, and nodded. "It does, indeed."

"I can't say we're very happy that you used our woman as a decoy." Morgan folded his arms and glared at Peter.

"We ought to beat the crap out of you for that one," Henry agreed.

"I didn't do it on purpose," Peter said. "Dennis was there, and she was about to walk into his arms anyway. I just told her when to make her move."

The dance had officially ended, and the lights had been raised. Samantha and her husbands had fussed over them all, while Ginny poured out cups of coffee.

Adam arrived back at the hall and made a beeline for his oldest brothers. "I ought to throw the both of you behind bars for that stunt you pulled tonight."

Tamara sipped her coffee and watched the way Ginny's gaze urgently swept over Adam. She sighed when she saw that he was safe and sound. Ginny must have sensed Tamara's scrutiny because the young woman met her gaze, blushed, and then looked away.

"What stunt would that be? I just happened to catch—"

"Don't pull that shit on me. You 'just happened,' my ass. I *just happened* to find the little trip wire you installed." Adam walked right up and got in Morgan's face. "You should have told me what was going on, so I could have been there for you."

"You *were* there for me. That was you I saw cuffing Preston Rogers, wasn't it?"

"After the fact. If it weren't for Peter's having alerted me—" Adam walked off, clearly at a temporary loss for words. No one made a sound or so much as twitched. Tamara didn't think she'd ever seen a man as angry as Adam Kendall was at that moment. He exhaled deeply and turned back to face his brothers.

"Look, I understand your mind-set. You thought, being the oldest, that you'd step up and step in and protect everyone else. But I'm the Sheriff of this town. This kind of thing is my *job*, and when you bypassed me, you diminished that job, and me."

Morgan exhaled. "Christ, that's the last thing I meant to do. But you're right, and I'm sorry."

Clearly an apology wasn't what Adam had expected because he looked astounded. But since it had been offered, he nodded. "Okay, then. Good."

He turned his attention to Peter. "How are you doing, G-man?"

"I'm okay. Just got nicked when Jimmy's shot went wide is all."

"Yours didn't go wide, but you didn't kill him, either. He's on his way to Waco by ambulance, with a state trooper riding along as escort."

"Good."

Tamara looked from her men, to Peter. "So now that everyone's here, does someone want to tell us what the heck that was all about? And how did you know to come to the rescue?"

"Preston Rogers and his motley crew have been distributing drugs in concert with a very nasty slimebucket south of the border named

Miguel Ramos, who deals drugs, arms, and humans. We've known about Rogers for some time, but could never really prove anything."

"I thought the Piper was too small to be used transporting drugs," Tamara said.

"They didn't use the Piper for the drugs, they used it to exchange the money and set the deals in motion. Then about four months ago, Ramos demanded to be paid in uncut diamonds, and the pilot and owner of the Piper saw his chance. He faked a crash, hid the plane, hoping to cash in."

"Only Rogers found out about it?" Morgan guessed.

"Exactly. We had some good information that he needed to find that Piper ASAP because Ramos doesn't like to be crossed. Anyway, we located the plane and found the diamonds. Then I put in the tracker and the bug—which was how I knew you needed help—and then waited to see if Rogers would come after it and incriminate himself."

"Which he did in a very large way," Henry said.

"I'd say so, yes," Peter said.

"Well, hell's bells." Uncle Goodwin huffed out a breath and got to his feet. "You'll want to take that Piper as evidence." He shook his head then met Tamara's gaze. "Guess we're back at square one in our business venture." And then he smiled.

"Guess so," she agreed, and very sneakily checked Morgan and Henry's reaction to that statement in her peripheral vision.

"Not necessarily," Morgan said. Then he straightened from where he'd been lounging against one of the tables and held his hand out to Tamara. "Let's go home, Red, and…talk mergers."

Chapter 20

"Now that we're alone…" Morgan's sentence drifted off, punctuated by the sound of the front door closing.

Tamara, who'd preceded both men into the cottage, turned to face him, intent on asking him to finish what she hoped was a very personal, very sexy proposition.

Instead, there they stood, her two handsome flyboys. Shoulder to shoulder, arms folded in front of their chests, they wore twin murderous expressions directed at her.

Fighting to hold back her smile, she copied their pose. "Yes? Now that we're alone?"

"Do you have *any* idea how utterly terrified we were when Dennis dragged you through that door tonight?" Morgan's voice had softened. Tamara figured that was probably a bad sign.

"We've a good mind to turn you over our knees and paddle the living daylights out of you." Henry, who could usually be counted on to be adorably charming, looked as if he would gladly chew nails right then.

Oh, they both looked as if they were at the very ends of their ropes. It didn't take any effort at all to imagine just how lethal these two Kendalls could be when the occasion demanded. Dennis didn't know how lucky he was that neither of her men had gotten his hands on him.

Tamara's own personal revelation of earlier that evening—that she was all the way in love with these two men—still felt fresh and new and a little bit scary. What didn't feel scary was Henry's threat, or the forbidding expressions on each of their faces.

So she inhaled deeply, exhaled, and strived for an insouciant attitude. "Is that a fact?"

"Yes, that is a fact." Morgan frowned even as his gaze speared her.

He's wondering what I'm thinking and why I don't seem to be worried. She decided not to let them wonder for too long. A part of her realized she stood on a precipice. This would be the moment when everything changed. Tamara knew she'd remember this moment for the rest of her life.

She'd never said the words to any man in her entire life, never even imagined that she would ever want to say them. Yet here she was about to say them to two men. Tamara didn't let herself angst over the decision she'd made, and she sure as hell didn't let herself worry that they didn't feel the same way about her.

They'd damn well better love her back, or she was going to clobber them both.

Just jump right in, both feet, one bold move. "Do the two of *you* have any idea how terrified I was, knowing the men I loved were facing God knows what, and there I sat, hiding in the bushes, powerless to help?"

"You've never been powerless." Morgan said the words instantly and convincingly. He relaxed his stance. His arms slipped to his sides and he took one step forward.

"I felt that way, tonight. When Henry skulked off to go to you, and I realized the kind of danger you could both have been in, I *felt* powerless."

"Just out of curiosity," Henry also relaxed and took a step forward, "what did you do to poor Dennis?"

That he would call the villain "poor Dennis" told her Henry's temper had completely dissipated.

"I stabbed him in the leg with a screwdriver."

"A screwdriver?" Henry repeated as if he'd never heard the words before. Since he looked dumbfounded, she decided to play it up. After all, she *was* a smart-ass.

"Uh-huh. A small, *itty-bitty* one about this big." She held her fingers apart to approximate the size of her weapon.

Morgan and Henry looked at each other, and she thought they might have paled, just a little. Morgan said, "Not *even* a fucking shovel."

"We'll have to tell Colt and Ryder how lucky they were that Susan, at least, was armed with a shovel."

That exchange completely confused Tamara. But she didn't worry about it, because just then both men turned their attention back to her as they each took one more step closer to her.

"Say it, please," Morgan said. "We both very badly need to hear you say the words."

"I will, but only if I get to hear them back." Tamara resisted the urge to pout.

"Red." Morgan crossed his arms in front of his chest again, and damned if the arrogant pose didn't turn her on.

Tamara shook her head. "You are *such* an alpha male. I always thought I was too smart to fall for one of those." She met his gaze, held it, and then met Henry's. "And here, I've fallen in love with not one, but two Alphas."

Neither man moved, and Tamara smiled. Alphas and arrogant, yes. And most definitely hers.

"I love you. I love you both. Although I'm not altogether certain how that happened."

Henry tilted his head to one side. "Well, we are pretty irresistible," he said.

Tamara laughed. She bet that smile of his had always allowed him to get away with the most outrageous things.

"But then, so are you." Morgan reached out one finger and stroked her face. "The moment I wrapped my arms around you that first time, I knew I was a goner."

"You make it sound like I'm a disease, and flyboy," she poked him in the chest, "I still haven't heard the words back."

"I love you." Morgan reached for her and drew her into his arms. "With everything that's in me, I love you." He kissed her, his lips warm and firm and oh, so delicious. His flavor seeped into her and brought her to that place of sanctuary between them. His tongue, bold and strong, caressed hers, drank from her and healed her.

Morgan ended the kiss gently and met her gaze. His lips spread into a half smile that melted her heart.

Henry pressed close to her and ran his hand down the back of her head. She turned to him and marveled at the way his eyes seemed to just sparkle.

"I love you, Tamara. You're my very heart, and the center of my world. I love you." He slipped his arm around her, lowered his head, and laid his lips on hers.

Wet and wild, he drew her in, drew her deep, so that Tamara wanted nothing more than to meld with him completely. Unable to resist him, she reached up with one hand and caressed his face. Her other hand blindly sought Morgan. When that man laced his fingers with hers, brought her hand to his mouth and kissed it, Tamara knew she'd come home.

"If you ever stop loving me…"

"Hush." Morgan stroked her arm. "We won't. That's not how Kendalls do things, baby."

"You're stuck with us," Henry said. "Good and stuck for the rest of your life. No going back, sweetheart. Not for any of us."

"I don't want to go back." Tamara blinked, trying to push back the tears determined to fall. "Oh, God, I don't want to go back. I need you both so much. You're the center of my world, too. My heart."

"Will you be the center of us now? Will you let us both inside you?" Morgan's voice shook, and Tamara knew it wasn't only the physical longing he felt.

The emotions of this moment, this sacred moment, shook them, hearts and souls, as it settled deeply and became their new core reality.

"Yes. Oh, yes, I want you both in me at the same time. I want us to be one flesh." She needed to connect with both her lovers at the same moment—in that blissful place they could only ever go—together.

Other times, they'd each carried her up these stairs, intent on seduction. This time she walked, showing them without words she needed no seduction. They belonged to her as surely as she belonged to them.

She'd never believed in a forever kind of love before meeting these two men. Now, she not only believed, she dared to claim it for herself, for them all.

They'd left a soft light burning, a lover's promise to return. Now that light played against flesh, against movements sinuous and seductive as clothing fell away, discarded, as hands and mouths explored.

"You're ours." Henry's heated words bathed her neck even as his hands cupped and kneaded her breasts. "Forever, sweetheart. You're ours, forever."

"And you're mine, both of you. Forever."

"Oh yes. We're all in this together, babe. You'll marry us and have our children. And we'll share grandchildren and, God willing, great-grandchildren." Morgan's proclamation could have been a vow.

Tamara reveled in their certainty, in the strength of their convictions and the strength of their hands. "I think I love your arrogance."

"Of course you do," Henry said.

Tastes and touches gave way to long, gliding sips and slow, sultry sighs. Her knees no longer held her. The men brought her down to the bed then stretched themselves out on either side—Morgan on her right, Henry on her left.

While they kissed and cupped and suckled, she fisted and squeezed and stroked. These men had the power to melt her bones, and it thrilled her to be able to command arousal in them both in turn.

She arched as Morgan nuzzled her breast and sucked her nipple into his mouth. Electric sensations of ecstasy swirled through her body. She felt her own moisture when Henry reached down and stroked her slit.

"Oh, yes!" Such pleasure swamped her when he speared his fingers into her pussy, and when he began to fuck them in and out of her, her hips moved, a needy cadence that begged for more, for a larger possession.

"You're so hot for us," Henry marveled. "So hot and wet."

"I crave you." No other word fit. "I hunger for your touch, for your hands and mouths and cocks. It's never been like this before."

"It's because we're mates," Morgan said. "The three of us, we're mates." He lifted his head so that their gazes connected. "It's more than I ever imagined it would be. Deeper. More primal, and more fulfilling. I love you, Tamara. Now and forever."

"I love you. I never believed in forever. But you've both made me a believer."

"Come here, love." Henry reached for her then and wrapped his arms around her. The press of his body, hot, vibrant male pushed her arousal higher. Her hips moved, bringing her clit closer to his cock, an instinctive move that sent shivers down her back when she felt the resulting slide of that engorged flesh between her wet folds.

"Put a condom on me, sweetheart."

"I will. But first…" She trailed kisses down his chest, sipping at the glistening sweat, relishing the saltiness of him, the heat of him.

She knew it was desire for her that coated him, and she wanted to drink in his desire in every way possible.

Her fingers followed the path of her lips. He shivered, and she smiled, the knowledge that she could affect such a strong man a warming balm to her soul.

On her hands and knees, she continued to sample him until his light shivers became great quakes, until his fingers combed through her hair, flexed, and gripped.

"You're killing me," he groaned.

Her laughter, low and sultry, brushed his scrotum. The scent of him there thrilled her, made her mouth water and her pussy gush. Another time, maybe she'd restrain him and drive him slowly insane. Right now, she needed his wonderful cock in her pussy, filling her.

She reached over to the bedside table and took out two condoms. She kissed the tip of Henry's cock just before she slid the latex in place.

Morgan hovered close, the heat of his body a blanket against her back and side, the rasp of his breathing a reassurance that while she touched only one lover, she aroused them both.

She turned her head and captured his cock with her mouth. He sucked in air, grabbed her head, and pumped his hips, fucking her mouth with deep, needy strokes.

The wet plop of her release of him echoed in the room. In moments, she'd smoothed the condom over him.

"Enough teasing." Henry grabbed her waist, lifted her, and brought her down on his cock.

"Mm, yes." Tamara sighed as Henry's penis entered her, as the heat and the strength of him filled her completely. Her entire body tingled with the thrill of him, with excitement born of the reality that her two lovers would soon both be inside her.

She moved on him, riding him in a gentle, thorough motion that drew the pleasure out, made it sharp and sweet.

Morgan ran his hand up and down her back.

"It turns me on to see you fuck him." His voice rasped, and his hand trembled.

Tamara looked over her shoulder and gave him what felt like a very wicked smile. "Fuck my ass," she begged.

"Oh, yes." His voice sent shivers down her spine, the dark timbre reverberating in her belly and sending out tiny fissures of electric excitement. He reached over her to the table for the lube.

She watched Morgan as she rode Henry while his fingers plucked and pinched her nipples.

When Morgan reached toward her, she hissed with the sensation of the cool, silky gel being smoothed over her anus. Her pussy clenched in anticipation, and she moaned just a little as she lowered her chest to Henry's so that she could raise her ass in invitation to Morgan.

"Mm, I think your ass is as hungry as your cunt." He sank one finger into her. She felt full, wicked, and wanton. She moaned and pushed her ass against that finger, then down, so she could rub her clit against Henry's groin.

"Yes, it is. Please, fuck me."

"Oh, don't worry, Red. I'm going to fuck you hard and fast and deep."

"Relax on me, Itty." Henry ran his hands over her back and caressed the back of her head. "Lie here and just let go."

Tamara nestled closer to Henry. Her heart thumped when Morgan grabbed her ass, when he spread her cheeks just a little. Oh, the heat of his cock, just the latex-covered tip of it as he pressed against her anus! She could only close her eyes and hum in pleasure as he pushed, as he began his penetration. The burning of his entry fueled her arousal, and she clenched her pelvic floor muscles, a reaction she couldn't prevent.

"Mm," Henry said. "I love it when you do that."

"I love it, too." Tamara sucked in a breath as burning edged into a sharp pain, as her anus stretched until she felt Morgan's cock enter her.

They both groaned as he slowly sank all the way into her.

"Oh, God." She felt full to bursting, yet at the same time completely free and alive.

"Easy, Red." Morgan moved in her, his thrusts slow and measured. It felt so damn good she could only make throaty sounds. Words seemed impossible.

She wanted the pleasure to last, wanted the slow climb to continue. A shiver coursed down her spine, wrapped around her, and tickled the edge of her clit. Deep inside she felt a curl, a spasm, felt the heat increase and her heart pound. Like a flower unfurling in the summer sun, her orgasm began to bloom. Unstoppable, nearly immeasurable, it grew and expanded beyond her ability to control, to prolong.

Tamara cried out as the sensations grabbed her. Her hips began to pump, to work the cocks within her, the motions sweet and sharp and sexy.

"Oh, oh, oh…" She could only take it as the climax flooded her, she could only take the pleasure and the thrills as they exploded up and through and out. Rapture tore her apart and put her back together, new, whole, fulfilled.

"Damn!" Morgan began to thrust in her, harder and faster. In and out, his hands gripping her as he, too, seemed captured by this bliss intent on possessing them all.

"Good God!" Henry thrust up inside her once, then again, and then held her tight as he emptied himself inside her. Through the echoes of her own ecstasy, she felt both men stiffen, felt the pulsing of the cocks inside her and the heat of the sperm as it filled the latex and pressed against her most sensitive places.

"Don't move." Morgan bore his weight on his arms on either side of her as he fought for breath.

"Don't worry." She doubted she'd move anytime in the next week.

Morgan chuckled then kissed her shoulder. He eased out of her and took a moment to caress her ass as he left the bed.

Tamara blinked, and the next thing she knew Morgan had returned. He gently cleaned her and then lifted her off his brother.

"Maybe I'll get you two to carry me everywhere."

"We could." Henry rolled off the bed. "Because, as I believe I've said at least once before, you don't weigh much."

He was back in moments, and then Tamara was in her new favorite place, between Morgan and Henry in this gigantic bed.

Morgan lay on her right, on his side so he faced her. His hand made lazy strokes down her body, a comforting caress that fed her emotions.

"You didn't answer us," he said.

"You didn't ask a question." She grinned at him, because she knew what he meant, and she knew she was right.

"She's right. We didn't ask," Henry said. "At least, not in so many words."

"And the words are important," Morgan said.

"Your words are important to me." Tamara reached up and caressed his face with one hand. He bent down and kissed her sweetly.

She lavished the same attention on Henry and received as tasty a reward.

"Will you be our partner, in business and in life? Will you marry us, have children with us, and grow old with us?"

Tamara's heart felt so full, she wondered it didn't burst. She'd never believed in love, or forever, but she did now.

"I can think of nothing better than to spend the rest of my life in love under two flyboys."

Morgan's hand stroked her stomach. "That's good. Because I have a feeling you're going to be spending a lot of time under us—or between us."

Henry grinned. "It's like I said that first day. Something falls out of the sky onto your land, it's yours."

"You did say that." Tamara smiled right back at him. "But I'm not certain that it's a law or anything."

"Don't you worry about it, Itty," Henry said. "We'll bring it up at the next meeting of the Town Trust."

"Good thinking," Morgan said. "That way if it isn't a law, it will be."

Tamara thought that sounded like a very good idea.

Chapter 21

"Are there going to be gun-toting villains at this party, too?"

Morgan laughed and then hugged her. Considering how the last party she'd attended in Lusty turned out, Tamara thought it had been a reasonable question to ask. She shook her head. Was that only two weeks ago? Time had been moving fast and furious since that night.

She'd never been busier, and she'd never been happier.

"It would seem the latest Lusty, Texas tradition is to have a casual engagement party at Kelsey Benedict's restaurant," Henry said as they stepped into Lusty Appetites.

"I think it's a great idea." Tamara looked around at how many people had already arrived. "But I do notice that neither one of you answered my question."

"Well, I see Peter made it back from Dallas," Morgan said. "So if there are any gun-toting bad guys, we can all take comfort in the fact that we have our very own Fed on duty, right here."

"Mm, I don't think he's on duty." Henry said.

Tamara took a moment to consider the other newcomer to Lusty. He looked very comfortable sitting at a table surrounded by a couple of Kendalls and several Jessop and Benedict cousins. "At least now you know why you thought there was more to him than met the eye," she said to Morgan.

"Yes. Finding out he was a Fed was a relief, all things considered."

Just then Tracy Jessop came out of the kitchen carrying a tray of pastries. "Well, here are the guests of honor, at last!"

"We're not late," Morgan and Henry said that at the same time.

"Sure you are," Matthew Benedict called out. "And we all know why, too."

Tamara noticed her men grinned in response to the good-natured teasing and certainly didn't deny the implied accusation. She felt her face heat and could only shake her head. "Goodness, I'm going to be related to all these testosterone makers!" Having such a large extended family was going to take some getting used to. For a long time it had only been her and Goodwin.

Tracy set down the tray and nodded. "We are few, and they are many."

"You're going to come and sit with me, aren't you?" Tamara inflected a note of pleading in her voice. "You were, after all, the first woman friend I made here."

Tracy grinned. "Just as soon as I bring out the rest of the nibbles. Kelsey thought that for tonight we'd just set everything up like we do for the Sunday buffet and let everyone help themselves."

"That's an excellent idea," Henry said. "That way no one will necessarily know when I cop two of those wonderful cream things you make."

People started arriving in a steady stream soon after that. Morgan and Henry had secured Tamara a seat at the same table as Jake, Adam, Jordan, and Peter. Tracy came and sat next to her. Tamara wondered at the undercurrents she felt between her friend and both Peter and Jordan. She caught a bit of teasing, a bit of flirting, and a whole lot of covert looks—amongst all three of them.

She'd ask Morgan and Henry what they thought about that, later.

Tamara had to admit, she felt like a queen. Both her men waited on her hand and foot. Every new arrival came over to congratulate her and then ask her if she was certain she knew what she was letting herself in for, hooking up with these two flyboys.

Tamara kept smiling and let her men think what they would about her failure to correct anyone's pity.

As the evening progressed, she began to understand that this sort of pampering wasn't likely going to be a onetime thing. She spent some time watching the other young families around her. Matthew and Steven Benedict attended to Kelsey. There just was no other word that fit. Their brothers, Joshua and Alex, made certain Penelope was comfortable and wanted for nothing. One of them had his hand on her the entire time. The newlyweds arrived, relaxed and happy from their honeymoon. She doubted Colt or Ryder took their eyes off Susan for more than a moment during the entire evening, and neither one of them got more than a few steps away from her side.

Not only did none of the women seem to mind the concerted attention from their mates, they positively glowed. Tamara could certainly understand that. Her men made her feel special, something she'd not had much experience with in her life.

"Well now, what do you have to say for yourself, Morgan Kendall?"

Tamara hadn't seen the older woman approach. Morgan bent low to hug Kate Benedict, then stepped back and laughed. Tamara quickly got up to give the woman a hug. It amazed her how strong Grandma Kate's embrace could be.

It was hard not to notice that the conversation around them had hushed, just slightly.

"Me?" Morgan took Kate's hand and kissed it gallantly. "*I'm* not the one who correctly predicted, right here in this very restaurant, that the right woman for Henry and me would fall out of the sky. That's quite a talent you have there, Kate Benedict. So tell me, who are you going to turn your matchmaking talents on next?"

Kate's laughter, full of fun, seemed to ripple out and affect the entire party because everyone smiled at the sound.

Kate reached up and patted Morgan's cheek. "I'm not telling. That way, they can all be on their toes."

Morgan shook his head. "You're bad."

"I've earned the right," she said.

Just then the door opened and three men stepped into the restaurant. Tamara had never seen them before, but she had no doubt they were Benedicts. She'd bet they were triplets, too, although they weren't identical.

"We heard there was a party going on here," one of them said.

"Oh, my goodness! I didn't know if you'd make it in time, or not. Everyone, look what the wind blew all the way down from New York City!" Grandma Kate made her way over to the newcomers, each of whom hugged her in turn, each one lifting her off her feet as he did so.

"You must come over and meet our Tamara. She's engaged to Morgan and Henry. Tamara, this is Richard, Trevor, and Kevin Benedict. They're Carson, Michael, and Abigail's boys. They're moving back home. Isn't it grand?"

Tamara could see both her men were pleased with the arrival of their cousins. Kate went on to explain that they'd been in New York for the last few years, heading up the east coast branch of Benedict International, an investment and brokerage firm.

"Just what we need," Henry greeted them. "More Benedicts!"

"And more to come," one of them said. "The twins and Julia will both be here in another week."

Tamara knew her jaw dropped. "Your parents had a set of triplets *and* a set of twins?" She couldn't imagine having more than one child at a time.

"Actually," Richard said, "they had two more besides. There are seven of us all told."

"Sweetheart, did we mention that Kendalls tend to have large families, too?" Morgan asked.

He wore such teasing look, but she knew he wasn't kidding. "No, I think you were probably saving that bit of news for a special occasion," she said.

"When Carson told me you were all coming back to Lusty, I was thrilled," Kate said. "It'll be so nice having so many of my children and grandchildren close by."

"You're not globetrotting so much anymore, Grandma Kate?" Trevor asked.

"No, Grandma's got a new hobby," Joshua called out. "Marrying off her unattached grandchildren and associate grandchildren."

"Oh, go away with you." Kate laughed. "I'm just a senior citizen intent on enjoying her family."

Tamara doubted any in attendance actually believed that for one minute.

"Grandma's already two for two," Joshua said. "Alex and I have her to thank for our Penelope, and I don't know how, but I'm certain she arranged for Tamara to come to the flyboys, here."

"Well, I'm glad you're going to be here," Kevin said. "Maybe you can find a couple of husbands for Julia. Our baby sister has *way* too much time on her hands."

"Oh, I'm certain Julia is more than capable of finding her own soul mates," Kate said.

Morgan and Henry's parents arrived, and Samantha made a beeline straight for them.

"Have I told you how happy I am that I've finally got a daughter?" Samantha's declaration stunned her, and Tamara couldn't stop her eyes from tearing.

"Have I told you how happy I am to finally have a mother?" A collage of images and times past, times when she'd so desperately needed her mother, flashed through her mind. It had been her way to tough it out, to act as if it didn't matter, that emotional desertion of her parents.

Now she could admit the truth to herself. It had mattered, and it had hurt in a way that she understood now she'd never really dealt with.

"I'm glad," Samantha said. "I think you and I are going to be very close."

Tamara thought so, too.

Ginny Rose arrived with her son, Benny. The little guy seemed to just glow from all the attention the adults in the room lavished on him. He hugged the ladies and high-fived the men, but it was Adam and Jake Kendall whose attention he immediately sought.

Tamara caught the look Adam sent Ginny, and she wondered the restaurant didn't catch fire as a result. Jake's expression appeared no less incendiary. Ginny blushed, and immediately set about making herself useful.

"I wonder when the young'uns are going to make a move in that area?" Tamara felt certain Henry's whispered question didn't reach anyone but Morgan and her.

"Adam danced with her at the reception a couple weeks ago," she said.

"Mm, I did notice that, and I thought that was going to be the beginning of something."

She knew her men well enough to know their interest in the situation wasn't superficial. Family was vital to them both. Their roots went deep, all the way back to the 1880s and the founding of this town, named by their family's matriarch, Amanda Jessop-Kendall.

Since they were men, however, emotional situations sometimes confused them. Men and women were vastly different creatures. Tamara had been made privy to some of Ginny's story, and while she herself had never been in an abusive relationship with a man, it could be argued she'd been emotionally abused by her parents, with their neglect and their lack of love.

"Some women can never come back after they've been hurt." Because it was there, she laid her head on Henry's shoulder. His arm came around her, and Morgan laced the fingers of his right hand with her left. "I don't think that's going to be the case with Ginny. But the man—or men—who want to take her on will have to have a whole lot of patience."

"Well, one thing Adam has always had in abundance is patience. Jake, not so much so."

"I think Jake might surprise you, then. Because sometimes a man can transform himself, if he wants to badly enough."

"You're a pretty insightful woman, Tamara Jones. So tell me." Morgan brought her hand up to his lips and kissed it. "What do you see as our future?"

Tamara looked around at this large group of people, most of whom had already accepted her as family, and considered the future.

There would be marriages and babies. Good times, and most likely some hard times. There would be love and laughter and probably the odd round of fisticuffs.

Tamara and her two flyboys would live here, work here, and quite probably grow old here. And in the process they would weave a fabric of family and friends, a fine tapestry that would be strong enough to endure generation after generation.

She saw a future she never would have thought she could ask for but was oh, so very grateful would be hers.

She turned to Morgan, leaned closer and placed a chaste kiss on his lips. Then she turned her head and gave Henry a kiss, too.

"I see years of love, and laughter, and living. I see us, together, forever."

Who could ask for a better future than that?

THE END

HTTP://WWW.MORGANASHBURY.COM

ABOUT THE AUTHOR

Morgan Ashbury writing as Cara Covington.

Morgan has been a writer since she was first able to pick up a pen. In the beginning it was a hobby, a way to create a world of her own, and who could resist the allure of that? Then as she grew and matured, life got in the way, as life often does. She got married and had three children, and worked in the field of accounting, for that was the practical thing to do and the children did need to be fed. And all the time she was being practical, she would squirrel herself away on quiet Sunday afternoons, and write.

Most children are raised knowing the Ten Commandments and the Golden Rule. Morgan's children also learned the Paper Rule: thou shalt not throw out any paper that has thy mother's words upon it.

Believing in tradition, Morgan ensured that her children's children learned this rule, too.

Life threw Morgan a curve when, in 2002, she underwent emergency triple by-pass surgery. Second chances are to be cherished, and with the encouragement and support of her husband, Morgan decided to use hers to do what she'd always dreamed of doing: writing full time.

Morgan has always loved writing romance. It is the one genre that can incorporate every other genre within its pulsating heart. Romance showcases all that human kind can aspire to be. And, she admits, she's a sucker for a happy ending.

Morgan's favorite hobbies are reading, cooking, and traveling – though she would rather you didn't mention that last one to her husband. She has too much fun teasing him about having become a "Traveling Fool" of late.

Morgan lives in Southwestern Ontario with two cats that have attitude, a dog that has no dignity, and her husband of thirty-nine years, David.

Also by Cara Covington

Ménage Everlasting: The Lost Collection: *Love Under Two Gunslingers*
Ménage Everlasting: The Lost Collection: *Love Under Two Lawmen*
Ménage Everlasting: Lusty, Texas 1: *Love Under Two Benedicts*
Ménage Everlasting: Lusty, Texas 2: *Love Under Two Wildcatters*
Ménage Everlasting: Lusty, Texas 3: *Love Under Two Honchos*
Ménage Everlasting: Lusty, Texas 5: *Love Under Two Strong Men*

Also by Morgan Ashbury

Siren Classic: Song of the Sirens 1: *The Seductress*
Ménage Amour: Song of the Sirens 2: *The Enchantress*
Siren Classic: Songs of the Sirens 3: *The Beauty*
Siren Classic: Magic and Love 1: *The Prince and the Single Mom*
Siren Classic: Magic and Love 2: *The Princess and the Bodyguard*
Siren Classic: Magic and Love 3: *A Prince for Sophie*
Siren Classic: A Siren Adult Fairy Tale: *Beau and the Lady Beast*
Ménage Amour: Reckless and Brazen 1: *Reckless Abandon*
Ménage Amour: Reckless and Brazen 2: *Brazen Seduction*
Ménage Amour: Shackled and Shameless,
A Reckless Abandon Novel: *Shackled*
Siren Classic: *Lily in Bloom*
Siren Classic: *Made for Each Other*
Ménage Amour: *The Lady Makes Three*
Ménage Amour: *Wanton Wager*
Ménage Amour: *Cowboy Cravings*
BookStrand Mainstream: *A Little R & R*

Available at
BOOKSTRAND.COM

Siren Publishing, Inc.
www.SirenPublishing.com